The Fly Man Murders

The Fly Man Murders

Mildred Davis
with
Katherine and Ren Roome

To order additional copies of this book or other books by the authors, contact:

HARK LLC

www.harkpublishing.com

To Ty, Zach, Ren, Emily, Whit, Griff, Annie and Claire

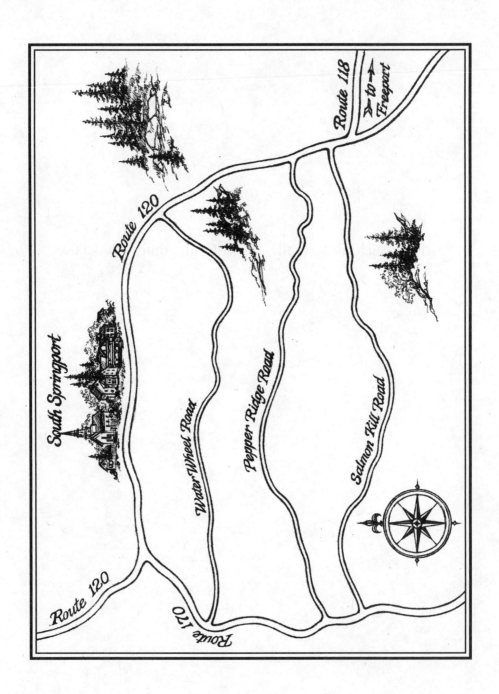

Prologue

"What was that?"

Beneath the roar of the low flying helicopter, the barking of the dogs, and the staccato bursts of the police radios, the two state troopers heard a nearby animal squealing.

They directed their flashlight beams into the thickly wooded paths that stitched back and forth across the camping ground. At first they saw only the placid ocean glinting through the spruce tree trunks but then, as the police helicopter spiraled northward driving gusts of wind down into the trees and underbrush, they spotted an apparition, a dwarf sized form so decaled with twigs and leaves it resembled a mythical creature. A miniature Caliban. For a moment it was pinned in the vaporous halo of the flashlights, and from its small throat came a moan, as of some primeval species waiting for the wolves to close in for the kill. It removed its grubby paws from its face to reveal eyes blind with terror, a mouth stretched into a black hole. At the sight of the two troopers, the creature was momentarily immobilized, but then it spun around to escape.

The two men sprinted after it. It gained the other side of the bridge and nearly reached the woods before one of them was able to lay hands on the small maddened thing.

"Hey, take it easy, kid. We're on your side."

It shrieked and kicked as they picked it up and headed back to the parking lot. One of the men spoke into his radio, and when they reached the parking lot, it swarmed with police cars, fire trucks, television trucks with antennae poking up like above ground periscopes, uniformed and plainclothes police and firemen, national guardsmen, public service employees, volunteer search parties, journalists and TV reporters. Police dogs leaped and pulled against their leashes. Trucks, SUVs, ordinary cars and motorcycles filled every available space in the lot.

"– fearing another strike by the 'fly' killer," an eager, almost jovial TV reporter was shrilling into her microphone, "representatives of local, county and state enforcement agencies, assisted by volunteers, have been out in droves since last – hold it! There's been a new development! Something's happening!" Her happy excitement was palpable. "I believe – yes, yes! They've found one of the children – "

"Hey, clear the way," the trooper was pleading. "Have a heart. We have to get this kid to his mother – "

At the word "Mother" the animal turned into a little boy. "Mama! Mama! Mama!" he bellowed.

The police cut a swath, elbowing reporters and photographers aside, and the troopers relinquished their find to a plainclothesman amid shouts of, "Which one is it? Is the kid hurt? Was he molested? Has he told you where the others are? What happened to him?"

Along with the child, four men piled into one of the police cars and, strobe lights turning, siren wailing, it angled out of the parking lot and headed out along the dirt road that led to the entrance of the camping ground. A convoy of official cars and media vans followed, while others remained behind to continue the search. Through it all, the small captive kept up his ear splitting lament.

They speeded along the dirt road through woods, fields, and then across a narrow causeway over a tidal inlet. The ocean off to the left of the car twinkled, a treasure trove of reflected jewels.

"Slow down," one of the men complained in a tired voice, "although wouldn't it be funny if we saved the kid from the maniac, only to kill him in a car crash?"

No one said anything but the driver slowed the car.

At the western edge of Freeport, the car skidded to a stop in front of a group of low-lying, institutional brick structures. The men hustled the child into the brightly lit police building, closing the door behind them and stationing guards to keep out their pursuers. The moment they were inside, the child stopped screeching and collapsed. A quivering mass of jelly, he rested his head against the chest of the policeman who held him. His eyes were blank and his facial muscles, under coats of mud and leaves, were loose. From outdoors came the din of the media, but inside it was oddly tranquil, as if they had entered a sheltered cove after being buffeted by a turbulent sea.

"There's no answer at the Haskell house," the desk sergeant said. "They must be out searching on their own. I left a message on their machine."

As the police officer placed the child on the wooden bench opposite the sergeant's raised desk, another man appeared and knelt in front of the small boy.

"I'm Captain Rohman, son. What's your name?"

From a whirling dervish the child had metamorphosed into a dirty vegetable. He stared past the captain and showed no reaction to the question. Intermittently he stirred, but only to bring a little fist up to wipe his nose. The captain reached into his pocket and offered him a handkerchief. The child shrank away.

"Tell us what happened, son."

This time the head lifted, giving everyone in the room a view of a face more swamped with misery than any one of them had ever witnessed. A policeman blew his nose.

"Bobby," the little boy whispered.

"Is that your name? You're Bobby Unger? Okay, Bobby, tell us what happened."

His voice heart broken, the child wailed, "Don't tell Mama!"

"Don't tell Mama?" Tension, perplexity and compassion warred on the captain's face. "Where *is* your mama, Bobby? Wasn't she with you?"

The dismal little figure humped itself into a ball and moved back against the wall. It seemed to be burrowing, looking for a crack behind the bench into which it could disappear. A paroxysm shook the small frame and a single excruciating sob broke from the throat. Around the room, stolid faces, accustomed to viewing tragedies on a day-to-day basis, were making visible efforts to remain rigid.

"Bobby, you have to help us find the others."

No response.

One of the uniformed men reached into a pocket and produced a lint coated lemon drop. He brushed it off with his fingers and held it out on the palm of his hand. The little boy looked at it for a moment and then, with a swipe of his hand, knocked it to the floor.

"You thirsty, Bobby? Want a drink?"

No response.

"Tell us where you were camping, Bobby. Were you pretending to be cowboys rounding up the cattle?"

This time when the boy raised his face, a child peered out of an old man's eyes.

"Maybe you pitched your tent next to a stream. Cowboys always do that. Can you help us find the stream, Bobby?"

Suddenly the child screamed, "Stop calling me Bobby! I'm not Bobby. I'm Teddy!"

Confused, the captain looked around for help. None was forthcoming. "I thought when you said Bobby before – "

A chest-ripping sob.

"Listen, Teddy, we have to find Bobby and his mother. We need your help. You went camping Friday with your friend Bobby – that right? And his mother. You were expected home yesterday morning but you never showed. What happened?"

The expression on the boy's face made the captain falter. He rubbed his palm against his nose. "You've got to tell us, Bo – Teddy. They may be in trouble."

A sob.

"Maybe if we go back to the campground."

The child turned his head towards the wall and his shoulders shook with uncontrollable, silent sobs.

"Want something to eat, Teddy? Want a drink?"

"I wanna' be dead."

The room was quiet. Everyone stared unbelievingly at a four year old who wanted to be dead. The telephone rang. "South Springport Police . . . How long? . . . See anybody inside? . . . Name and address? . . . I'll send somebody right over."

He turned to a uniformed policewoman. "Party of the name of Lavenburg, corner of Upper Mast Landing Road and Bow, says a suspicious gray minivan's been parked down the road from her house for six hours. Take a look."

"How can a minivan be suspicious?" grumbled the policewoman. Obviously reluctant to leave the scene, she shoved a cap on her head and opened the door. Immediately, like the blast of a storm, shouts and questions hurtled into the station house. Before she could slam the door shut, the pandemonium grew even louder. A horn honked, tires squealed and two people – three, if you counted the object bouncing in a sling on the woman's chest – burst into the room. It required the combined efforts of four policemen to close the door after them.

"Mama!" little Teddy screamed. The woman flew across the room to scoop the boy into her arms. The baby howled, the woman sobbed, the chaos rose.

"Teddy, Teddy darling. Teddy, my darling, are you all right? Are you hurt? Oh Teddy darling."

She tried to pry him off the bench but suddenly he shrank away and hid his face. His father, tears streaming down his cheeks, forcibly lifted his son into his arms. "Are you okay, honey? Did anyone hurt you?"

Amid the babble and the confusion, Teddy lay quiescent against his father's chest. After his initial cry of "Mama!" he was like a rag doll, his eyes dulled by grief. His father hugged and kissed him repeatedly, the tears falling on the boy's head. They paid no attention to the others in the room. The baby continued to howl.

"Darling," his mother said when she was able to control her voice, "What happened? Where were you? We expected you back yesterday morning.

Where are Bobby and his mother?"

Without warning, the little boy vomited, spilling the contents of his stomach over the front of his father's shirt. His father hugged him closer as the small boy began retching out words. "Mama, Daddy, Mama, Daddy, Mama, Daddy – "

A policeman disappeared and returned with wet paper toweling and a glass of water. Teddy's father was completely oblivious to the other man's efforts to clean off his shirt.

"Mama, Daddy, Bobby screamed and screamed. He begged somebody to help. And the man – the man – Mama, Daddy. Bobby screamed and begged and when the man wasn't looking I ran away. I didn't help. I ran away. And Bobby begged and begged . . . ."

ONE

Wednesday, June 6
Faith

Overhead, in a tangled smudge of greens resembling a Pissarro painting – what did *I* know about Pissarro paintings? – a sparrow hopped from an upper to a lower branch to inspect a foreign looking object lying on the bench below. Me.

Holding on to the hard wooden slats, I started to sit up, but pain sizzled through my head and I fell back again. My foot struck something soft and yielding.

"Hey, Cunt. Watch it."

I rested before making another attempt. A squirrel skittered to the ground, sat up on its haunches and regarded me hopefully. I felt in my pockets, found no food and shook my head.

On the next try I managed to haul myself to a sitting position. First, I studied the corrugated bark on the oak tree and then I studied myself. What I could see was a black rayon jacket, a yellowed blouse and a rusty looking long black skirt. On my feet were cracked brown boots. My finger nails were black and the skin on the back of my hands was as corrugated as the bark.

"Basically, growing up, I was indulged with the wrong crowd. Know what I'm sayin'? I didn't do nothin'. I was framed."

I tried to see who was speaking but the sudden movement made the world begin to revolve.

"Fuckin' lawyer didn't do a thing. I did two years time for nothin'."

I was sharing the bench with a man who was wearing pin-striped dress trousers tied around the waist with a rope. His orange sweater had been knitted with a freak in mind; the sleeves were twice as long as his arms but the rest of it was so short it left his midriff bare. He wore maroon bedroom slippers.

"Gimme a dollah?"

I began searching for my leather pouch and the dizziness overcame me again. I put my hand to my head. A huge round knob protruded from the left side.

"You gonna' give me a dollah?"

I looked under the bench and then I patted myself like a policeman frisking a suspect. In my jacket pocket, nestled among crumbs and fluff, I found a dime. I handed it to my bench mate, the falsely accused ex con.

"That all you got?"

"I must've been robbed. Also hit on the head." I shut my eyes. When I reopened them, he was gone, along with the sparrow and the squirrel. But the leaves remained, sharp and clear against the brightening sky. Holding on to the bench, I got up and waited for the whirling world to steady itself. People slid by as if on one of those slow moving Christmas displays in store windows: a woman with an expensive hair cut, a leather brief case and jogging shoes; a pony tailed jogger in a pink tee shirt and purple shorts with ear phones clamped to her head; a black woman pushing a white baby in a stroller; two elderly females in pastel linen blouses and slacks and white sneakers; a boy on roller blades. It occurred to me that everyone in sight was wearing sneakers except for the boy and me.

I crossed a street into a more formal garden and followed the paths until I came to a pond. A boat half filled with a mix of children and adults, with a gigantic plastic swan attached to the back as if in hot pursuit, glided by. It was familiar and peculiar at the same time.

On the far side of the pond stood an artist with his easel. He was looking in my direction as he dabbed the canvas. My view was momentarily obscured by a heavily made up woman with huge masses of curly black hair, wearing a colorful gypsy costume and feeding pigeons who roosted on her head, shoulders and arms. She didn't appear to belong to the park, the present century or, in fact, this planet.

I circled the pond in order to observe the artist at work. It was true he had been looking in my direction because there was the bench and the gnarled tree. What was missing was me. Possibly I didn't exist.

The artist, too, appeared to be on the outer edges of substantiality. From his colorless hair to his pasty complexion and his khaki clothes, he seemed translucent and nearly not there. When he noticed me, he laid down his brush, reached into his trousers and held out two quarters. I accepted them, surprised by how hard and real the coins felt in my hand.

A woman, her face a crisscrossed map of misery, rooted about in a trash can. I waited until, with a furtive glance towards me, she scuttled off to the next trashcan. Competition among losers could be just as fierce as among investment bankers I thought, and then wondered how I knew about investment bankers. I did my own scrabbling in the trashcan until I found an empty orange juice container. I preferred milk cartons as they were less sticky and smelly but beggars, of course, could not be choosers. I ripped the top off, sat down on a nearby bench, and held it out in front of me. Occasionally, a passerby dropped a coin in.

In a playground confettied with children, I watched two of them climb a wooden structure. Their caretakers sat on benches, their conversation intermittently punctuated by rescue missions. But most of the time, they paid little attention to their charges. "You ought to take better care of them," I said. Open mouthed, they stared at me and then turned away.

I was back on the street. A man sitting on the sidewalk held a sign that read, "I AM A 55 YEAR OLD HANDICAPPED VIETNAM VETERAN WITH AIDS. CAN USE WORD AND EXCEL. PLEASE HELP ME." A short, concise and to the point resume. It seemed a worthier cause than that of the ex con, falsely accused or not, and I emptied my container into his.

Suppose I made up a sign of my own, I wondered, what would it say? I rubbed the protuberance on the side of my head to assist my thought processes but my brain was a traffic-clogged street with all ideas in gridlock.

Stopping at a flower and produce market, I surveyed the offerings: tulips, roses, carnations, lilies on one side; apples, oranges, bananas, kiwis, papayas, mangoes on the other.

"May I have an apple?" I asked the small, dark-eyed, dark-haired boy on sentry duty.

"Twenty-five cents."

"I gave all my money to a veteran."

He looked at me, started to shrug and then, after a hasty glance behind him towards the dark interior of the establishment, handed me an apple.

"Thank you." I walked on, eating. As if I were invisible, no one looked at me. The title of a book along those lines floated up into my consciousness but then floated back down before I could grab at it. A large group of rubber-neckers ringed an exhibit on the ground and I razored in to view the attraction. A large black man, bare chested and wearing dirty torn trousers, lay on the ground, his tin cup beside him, the coins spilled out. A medic stood over him with an IV bottle, the tube inserted into the unconscious man's arm. Two other medics were carrying a stretcher from a double-parked ambulance while four policemen stood by to offer assistance.

The Invisible Man, that was it. Now *here* was a man who was no longer invisible. I walked off.

A young woman with her long brown hair in a braid to her waist, dressed in a long peasant skirt and white peasant blouse came dancing by, whirling around with a small blond boy in her arms. The boy's face was serious but when she put him down on the ground, he reached up with his arms and pleaded, " 'gain, 'gain, Mommy."

Faintly dizzy, I sat back down on a bench. Coins rattled in my juice container. A young bearded man with torn jeans had dropped some quarters in. I totaled my net worth. Four dollars and twenty-five cents.

I had to save my money.

Why?

A whiff of fragrance, an inflection of a voice, a certain set of features sent spasms through my nerves as if blood clots intermittently dissolved, allowing trickles of memory to seep through. There was something I had to do. Some place I had to go.

I walked up a hill. A building, which I somehow knew to be the State House, loomed up on my left. I even knew, without looking, that at the top of the great golden dome, there was a weathervane in the shape of a fish. Why, I no longer recalled. I started down the hill on the other side, past an old church, a restaurant and a bar that, somehow, I knew served cheap beer. I passed a building where I knew that I often ate meals. I walked down Friend Street – where I had never yet found a friend – and arrived at a place called TD BankNorth Garden although there was nothing of a garden about it. I was in a train station. I saw a sign: Amtrak.

Swept along by the flow of humanity, I ended up beached on one of the ticket lines. When it was my turn, I said, "How much is a ticket to – " and waited for a name to appear on the screen of my mind. The screen was blank.

"Where to?" the ticket seller asked impatiently. She was an attractive middle-aged woman with a smooth cap of black hair but her face was set in a permanent frown. Behind me a voice said, "Excuse me, Lady. I'm in a hurry." Somehow I was shunted aside. A man sprawled against the wall said, "I could use some bread" but I told him, "No more charity." Two needs gnawed at me – the need to go to the bathroom and the need to eat. First things first. Behind the door marked "Women", I waited on another line. Someone behind me grabbed a cubicle when it was my turn.

"You can't trust anybody," I said aloud.

The woman mopping the floor said, "You just learnin' that? At your age?"

Your age? What age was that?

After using the toilet, I went to the wall mirror to answer the question. The image resembled a cubist painting with each feature seen from a different angle. (What did *I* know about cubist paintings?)

I was back on the street. A man handed me a circular advertising automobile tires. What did he think I was going to do with an automobile tire? Make a swing? Raft down a river? I turned the circular over and on the other side were two blue and white photographs, one of a beautiful little girl and the other of a demented looking man.

"HAVE YOU SEEN US?"

The little girl's name was Daisie Lee Fawley. DOB 4/16/03. Height 3'5". Eyes gray. Hair brown. Wt. 38 lbs. Sex F. Date missing 05/5/07 from Denver, Colorado. Call 1-800-843-5678. National Center for Missing and Exploited Children.

Fire simmered in my stomach.

Perhaps the child was safe at home by now. Perhaps the man was a harmless friend. Perhaps the whole thing was nothing but a custody battle.

Or perhaps —

I walked back a few blocks to the place where I knew I could get a meal. Decades ago, it had been a school. Every surface which required paint lacked it, and every fixture capable of rusting was rusted. I went past an office occupied by a black man staring at a blank computer screen, a library that I knew was full of paperbacks with torn covers and missing pages, a thrift shop with racks of faded and stained clothes, and headed for the dining room. It was a large room with cement block walls and long, metal tables that may have been there since school children sat at them in the 1950s. The noise of several hundred people scraping metal chairs on worn linoleum was deafening.

The woman ladling out the stew was of a different species from those receiving it. The former was well bathed, well coiffed, well manicured, and well dressed. The latter, a checkerboard of black and white, male and female, old and young, wore formal suit jackets with torn jeans; sweat shirts with long skirts; jeweled blouses with shorts. One woman and her three little girls were decked out as if going to a secondhand party in tulle and chiffon. Every day was Halloween at the shelter. The children, looking around furtively while they ate, had the stamp of Third World refugees who had never had enough to eat, enough clothes meant for themselves alone, enough toys which hadn't belonged to someone else. Conversations bounced around me as I devoured my stew.

" . . . the world is going to end in between five point six million years or seven point four million years."

" . . . tell you straight up and down he was not the kind to get in trouble. A homebody person. Give him a video, he's okay."

"Weights. That's the ticket. You gotta' have at least twenty-five pound weights. Do it regular. You don't do it regular, it don't do you no good. One hour daily minimum, rain or shine. Trouble is where to get the weights."

" . . . took inventory on how I was motivating around the shelter. After my mother passed I couldn't find me permanent housing. I needed structure. My life was stagnated. I wasn't actually brought up that type of kid. There is the positive way and the insanity way. I talked to my counselor about my short-term goals. It's all about education."

"Arabs and Indians, they get the summer jobs. Guys from Hong Kong. I ask you. Just answer me. We're the silent majority. How come we're so fucked up?"

" . . . let him out in a coupla' years. Know what he does? Grabs a kid in the park and takes him home. Cops find the kid in a garbage bag a week later."

"What's your name?" a small boy next to me asked.

"Faith."

For a moment all sound was blocked out. The name hovered in midair and I didn't know where it had come from. It was as if a missing piece of a puzzle had dropped into the correct notch all by itself.

"Faith what?"

"I don't know."

"You don't know your own name?"

"Eat your dinner and shut up," the heavyset woman next to him instructed.

"I'm finished. I want more." The statement echoed from some long forgotten novel.

"They don't serve no seconds," the woman told him, and that too was an echo from the same novel, but not in those words.

I got on line for coffee.

"Black?" asked another attractive young woman: well bathed, well coiffed, well manicured.

I looked at my hands. "No, I'm white."

She didn't know whether to laugh or be serious. Compromising, she smiled. "Do you want your coffee black?"

"With cream and sugar please."

"Did you register at the front desk?" It was like the first day of school.

I sipped my coffee. "No."

"You ought to go to the office tomorrow first thing and register."

"Why?"

"So you can be tested and we can start you on a prog – "

"Tested for what?"

Slightly embarrassed, she said, "Well, you know. Uh – drugs, alcohol – "

I nodded and thanked her. Then, not telling her I had no time for programs and testing, I went down the corridor, like driftwood following the current, past small cluttered rooms where entire families lived, past dirty bathrooms, past laundry rooms until I came to the women's dormitory. Most of the cots were taken; footlockers at the bottom of them crammed with photographs, cosmetics, medicines and knick-knacks. I picked an unoccupied bed and sat down. Then, almost immediately, I jumped up and went out to find someone who looked official.

"What's today?" I asked.

"Wednesday, June sixth."

"What year?"

A passing resident said, "You sure fucked up, Lady."

"Two thousand seven."

Thoughts, like fireflies trapped in a jar, knocked futilely against the sides of my skull. Abruptly, the room seemed saturated with an effluvium of sweat and urine, and what was worse, the end of hope. The lighting was inadequate and the noise excessive. In addition, I couldn't breathe. And yet I knew, or sensed, that I had been living in places like this for years, if not happily, at least in a state of placid inertia. But now, for some reason I did not know, I had to leave this behind. It could not have been clearer to me.

Without knowing how I had arrived there, I was back on the streets, breathing deeply of the polluted air as if inhaling mountain breezes. Unlike that poor woman tied down by her three children, I could go anywhere, do anything. Well, almost anything.

I walked past bodies sprawled in doorways, past makeshift cardboard shelters, past shuffling derelicts. I found a bench and first sat, and then lay down on it. A recurrent scene kept flashing through my head: a train speeding past lettered station signs I couldn't read.

The world is going to end in between five point six million years and seven point four million years.

In that case, I had to hurry.

TWO

Thursday, June 7
Dilly

I waked up and looked at the sky. The shade was up. If sunny I gotta' go to the playground. If rainy, I get to play in my room. I hoped it rainy. Those guys in the playground grab a lot. I like to play in my room with my tractors.

Sunny. The playground.

I feeled for my tippie cup. No more juice. I cuddled Curious George. Was it daytime enough? Mommy says don't call until daytime. I called anyway.

She usually answers right away. Not this time. No footsteps down the hall. Usually she says, "Too early, Snoogums. Go back to sleep."

I yawned. I called some more. No answer.

I climbed down. I went in the hall to Mommy's room. Mommy's bed a mess but no Mommy.

I got really grumpy. I looked in the bathroom and the study and guest rooms, even basement. No Mommy. I beginned running. The bottoms of my pajamas so long they make me trip. I hurted my nose but I was brave. I didn't cry. I went to the glass next to the door. Mommy's Jeep Wagoneer in the driveway so she didn't go anyplace. She was here. Outside maybe.

Never go outside alone.

It was like Mommy talking inside my head. Not real, pretend. 'Magination. I turned the button on the front door and putted just my head outside.

"Mommy!" I was getting really grumpy. I yelled some more.

You having a tantrum, Dill Pickle?

"Yes! I'm having a tantrum!"

I tried to see down the road. The driveway turned too much. I couldn't see after the first turn. I climbed in my crib and throwed Curious George and Blanky on the carpet. I climbed down and lied next to them. I was thirsty. I dragged George and Blanky in the kitchen. I opened the 'frigerator. Milk and juice on top. I pulled the footstool and standed and pushed the milk back. I grabbed the juice. It crashed. Glass and juice all over the floor.

I get discouraged easy. Also frustrated. I taked the milk. It was for Mommy. She drinked skim, I drinked whole. Whole what? But the whole was too big. I taked the skim. Would it make me stop growing?

My pajamas had plastic bottoms so I could walk on the floor. Not get cut up. I holded the milk carefully and I standed on the stool and washed the tippie cup. Juice and milk don't mix. I poured milk. I hardly spilled much. I drinked it fast. Some tears got in the milk. Tears poison?

I putted the milk back on the low shelf. It gets bad if you leave it out. I taked a apple and closed the 'frigerator.

I sat on the floor on a dry spot and cried. Only a little bit. I eated the apple. It was pretty tasty.

"Who taking care of me?" I asked George. He didn't know. George is pretend. He's stuffed. I said, "I'm finished crying. You proud of me?"

I put the inside of the apple in the garbage and I wrapped a kitchen towel around my hand like Mommy and picked up pieces of glass and putted them in the garbage. A piece went in my hand. I seed blood through the towel. I turned on the water and holded my hand under. I drinked some water. I played with the water awhile. I wished I could climb on the counter. Sometimes Mommy puts me on the counter and lets me spray and float my Coast Guard boat.

I carried my stool to Mommy's bathroom and slided open the door to the cabinet.

Never take any pills without permission.

I didn't. Only Band Aids. I tried to tear off the cover but it didn't come. I taked tissues to cover my hand. When the blood stopped coming out, I went to my room and opened the drawer. I taked out underpants and shorts and a tee shirt. The shirt makes a "T". I putted the wet diaper in the pail. I only wear diapers at night. Mommy said it was okay to have accidents. I talked to Mommy while I dressed.

"Mommy, I peed. I didn't mean it. When I'm four, pretty soon, I won't pee in bed anymore."

I can do pretty many things. The underpants and shorts were easy but the shirt got stuck on my head and I yelled. It taked me probably an hour to get it over my head. I hated that. I putted on my fireman boots. No socks.

What should I do? Nobody telled me. I taked more food from the 'frigerator. A carrot and bread and chicken. It was in tin foil. I putted them on the counter.

The telephone ringed. I yelled, "Mommy!" and I runned to the telephone. I couldn't reach. I runned to get the stool. The telephone stopped.

I pulled pieces from the chicken. I didn't eat much skin. Mommy says skin not healthy but it tastes good and crunchy. I went to the door to give the skin to Sir. It's okay for dogs. I yelled for Sir but no answer. I seed little birds cheeping in the bushes outside the back window. I heared a helicopter. I waved. Nobody waved back. A yellow dog goed by. Not Sir. I wrapped the chicken back and putted it in the 'frigerator.

In my room, I taked the fire truck and the backhoe and the fork lift from the toy chest and made a ramp with the wood board on the toy chest to the floor. I attached the pintle pin at the back of the tow truck to a wagon and putted a little sailor in. It zoomed down the ramp. I spreaded the plastic sheet with the pretend town on the floor. It had a pretend garage and a library, a school and a hospital even. I zoomed the ambulance up and down the streets. Zing, zong, thonk, out on the highway.

I goed to the door to check. No Mommy. Where she go? A walk? Maybe Susie picked her up and they goed to lunch. They forgot I'm not in nursery school. Probably they thought Cindy was babysitting me. Maybe they be home any minute. I opened the door and went outside.

Never go outside alone.

I smelled the flowers in the stone flowerpots but they didn't have much smell. Mommy says they're panties. They don't look like panties. I sniffed the tree Mommy planted when I was born. Magnolia. It was even bigger than me. I went down the steps and tried to open the Jeep door.

Too heavy. I picked up pebbles from the driveway and throwed them. Not on the car. I filled my pocket with the prettiest. I might need them. I called "Sir!" No Sir. I throwed a stick but he didn't come to chase it. I looked a little way down the driveway.

Never go near the road without a grownup.

I can walk around the house. It isn't dangerous. I seed something in the pool. The pool needed vacuuming because of twigs and leaves. I picked up a stone and throwed it. A big black thing was in the water. It was furry and it floated. Did Mommy throw a stuffed bear in the pool by mistake? I didn't. I looked back at the house. See if Mommy back. The pool is dangerous. She be angry I went to the pool. No Mommy. It was okay to go on the top step of the pool. Even the second. I taked off the fireman boots and putted them on the side. I holded on tight to one step and tried to grab the furry thing. I couldn't reach. I finded a branch. I tried to push the furry thing with the branch. It didn't work. I had another idea. I laid down on my stomach on the side of the pool.

I reached. The furry thing moved. Something metal on the neck.

"Come here!" I said. It didn't. I got the skimmer. It was too heavy. I lied on my stomach again and holded the edge with one hand and reached. I couldn't. I went to the steps and reached. I holded on with one hand. Almost I could touch. I letted go of the side and reached with two hands. I falled in.

SKIP

I'm just like other kids. I love Mother and Father. They try to teach me what's right and what's wrong. They make sure I'll grow up and be a good person who's afraid of God and who always obeys the law. They want me to get good marks. They make sure I do my homework. I do chores around the house so I won't be lazy and get into trouble with drugs and things. I'm never rude and I never get impatient when I have to wait around for grownups to do things. I'm never afraid when I have to go home from school. I know if I'm good I won't get a beating. I love Mother and Father. I hardly ever get too many beatings when I'm good.

God, please help me.

THREE

Thursday, June 7
Faith

"Son of a bitch sold off the subsidiaries, fucked up the parent company and declared Chapter Eleven."

The two insomniac retirees, sitting side by side on the bench next to me, were dressed in fantastically colored spring flower hues – blue and green slickers, pink and lavender sport shirts, yellow and purple slacks. Only their sneakers were white and bland looking. "The chairman got the golden parachute and the rest of us got the shaft." It sounded like an oft-repeated litany. "Son of a bitch who bought the company reneged on my pension. Forty years building a company and I'm out on my ass."

"Why didn't you sue?"

"Now why didn't *I* think of that? Of course I sued. Trouble is the lawyer's a bigger crook than the leveraged buyout guy. Wouldn't take the case on contingency and charges me three hundred and fifty an hour. He's not a lawyer. He's a billing machine."

"There's no justice in the world."

There's no justice in the world.

"Damned right," I said, sitting up on my bench to address my neighbors. Needles pricked my arms and legs. Underfed sparrows and overfed pigeons cheeped and skittered in the early dawn light. The two retirees couldn't have looked more startled if one of the pigeons had spoken. They abruptly got to their feet and started walking away. "I have a big project this afternoon. Annie wants me to frame a picture for her."

And what was *my* project? And why wasn't I getting on with it? I checked my pocket to make sure the retirees hadn't swiped my savings, and then I hurried after them. Having misplaced my juice box, I held out my palm. The one who was shafted waved a dismissive hand at me, but the other gave me a quarter. As they walked off, I heard the shafted one say, "It'll only go for booze or crack. It's useless giving them money. Like sending food to Darfur. What we ought to do is distribute condoms."

Booze? Crack? What was crack? Where was Darfur?

A sign read, "Early Bird Special. $3.00. Orange juice, coffee, bagel with butter."

I was hungry. Were they hungry in Darfur? Would it be cheaper if I bought my bagel and orange juice in a store? Did they sell single bagels? Single glasses of orange juice? A cup of coffee? Ought I to go to a shelter for breakfast? Some didn't let you in until seven a.m. They were always after you to sign up for programs. Give them samples of blood and urine.

I went inside and ordered the special. The young Hispanic girl at the counter looked doubtful until I showed her twelve quarters.

"Tax," she said.

"Tax?"

"Oh, forget it," she said wearily.

I carried my special to a small table with chromium legs and a chipped Formica top. While I ate, I kept shaking my head to see if the loose parts would fall into place. Two women dressed in fluorescent tracksuits kept staring at me with what seemed like a combination of disgust and pity. One whispered something to the other and the second one nodded her head in emphatic agreement. They had definitely found common ground in their opinion of me. I thought of sticking out my tongue at them but refrained. I watched through the window as three boys in private school blazers and flannels walked by on the sidewalk. (How did *I* know they were private school blazers and flannels?)

I saved my Styrofoam coffee cup when I left the restaurant and rattled my few coins. An elderly woman holding a child's hand stopped. She handed the child something and he approached me. Half wary, half curious, he dropped the coins in my cup and continued staring.

"Come along," the woman said.

I stared back into the open, friendly face and I began to cry.

Alarmed, the little boy dashed back to the woman. Holding her hand as they walked off, he kept looking back to stare at me. I wished I had saved my napkin. As it was, I had to wipe my eyes with the bottom of my jacket. The coins rattled in my cup. Was crying a good sales pitch?

Although my mind didn't know what they were up to, my feet carried me along to my destination. My mind was occupied with a number of tableaux: a children's museum exhibit with names in one column, pictures in the other. Press the correct button and a light comes on. A statue without arms and a small voice at my side saying with assurance, "I bet *you* could fix it." A playground with sand castles. And a train station.

I was back at the Amtrak station.

I waited for a signal. Faces swirled past, footsteps echoed, voices shrilled. Doors in my head edged slightly open but slammed shut when I tried to wedge them wider.

Press the correct button and a light comes on.

I looked up at the departure board as if I were looking for a personal message directed only to me. And there it was: South Springport.

FOUR

Thursday, June 7
Dilly

The water comed over my head and I breathed it in my nose and mouth. I hated it. I wasn't brave. I kicked and I tried to cry but I swallowed water. I touched something. I picked up my head to get air but I couldn't find the top of the water. The thing I touched was furry. It moved. I feeled a step under my foot and I grabbed the fur hard and pulled. My nose comed out of the water a little bit and I breathed but I didn't know which way out. My toe slided in again. I didn't let go of the fur and I kicked hard and grabbed. I pulled myself on a step and got out of the pool. I coughed and some stuff comed out and I spitted. I cried a lot.

I watched the sky. No planes, no helicopters, no clouds even. When a bird flied by I yelled at him. I don't know why. When I couldn't yell any more I lied on the cement. It was warm. It feeled like it was raining inside my leg. I turned my head and looked at things from every day. Panties in the garden and seedum. But it wasn't like every day. It was like that Alice in Wonderland that Mommy readed me. I seed the movie. It was better than the book.

"Mommy! I won't be whiney. I promise. Come here!" I listened but no answer. I looked at the big window. No Mommy. I kicked the terrace. I yelled, "Mommy, Mommy, Mommy" until my mouth hurted. Also my feet from kicking. I looked at my hands. They had black hairs.

I knowed the hairs. I said, "Sir?" I runned to the pool but I stopped. I was careful. No falling in. I holded on to the sides and went down one step. The big furry thing against the steps. It moved back and forth like swimming. But it was only the water moving in the filter.

"Sir," I said, but no answer. "Sir, you dead?"

Two front paws and two back paws had wires. Why?

I was afraid. Actually, I wanted to hide. I walked backwards to the house until the edge of the terrace tripped me. I went inside. I leaved water on the floor. Mommy hates that. I sitted on the floor and pulled the boots off and water spilled on the rug. I putted the boots next to the door like Mommy says. I went to Mommy's bathroom and turned on the water in the tub. It was cold. I turned the other way until warm comed in. I plugged the bottom. I taked off the wet clothes and went inside the tub. I made the water some more warm. I lied back and my hair got wet.

It was wet anyway. My hands keeped me from going underneath. I goed back to my bathroom and got some of my bath toys. The beaver chewed on a log if you winded it.

The shark wiggled. I have lots of bath toys. All in a bag with holes hanging on a hook. But I like Mommy's bath better than mine. When my hands got wrinkled I climbed out of the tub and letted the water out. I dried on a towel. I stuffed the wet things in a hamper.

I picked out more shorts and a shirt. I can dress myself pretty well.

I eated more chicken. I looked outside the glass door. Mommy was right when she said never go near the pool alone. Some people believe God made the world. God is magic. Some people believe 'splosion. First 'splosion, then dinosaurs, then babies. I tried to bite a melon but it was too hard. Mommy said never play with a knife. I sitted on the floor and eated a peach. I didn't know what to do next. Nobody entertaining me. I was bored of this.

It's okay to go outside a little ways. I planted the peach pit so I'd have peaches for dinner. I slided on the slide. I didn't swing. Not by myself. I climbed to the tree house. Moore builded it for me. You have to be a good climber. I used the rope and the ladder. It holded four people, maybe six. It had a plastic roof in case of rain. I climbed down and went back to my room and zoomed my front-end loader. I writed a letter to Mommy. "Come home. Come home. Come home." I looked at the writing to see what it said. I couldn't read it. How mail it? I didn't know the address where she was. Maybe I could send it on Mommy's fax. I needed a number. Or I could use her computer but I don't know the magic words to make it go.

I made some pictures for Mommy. She says I show promise. I goed to the kitchen and taked sugarless gum from the box and teared off the paper. I chewed half and saved the other part for later. I went to Mommy's room and turned on the TV with the remote control. A lady said, "I glad you had excuse to come over." A man said, "Since when I need excuse?" I changed channels. Nothing good on. No construction. No trucks. I turned it off. Never leave TV on, Mommy said. The telephone ringed and I grabbed it off Mommy's table. I yelled, "Mommy!"

"May I speak to your mother, little girl?" a lady said.

"I'm a boy," I said.

"Get your mother," she said. She forgot to say please.

"I want my Mommy. *You* get her."

"Tell her come to the telephone."

"Mommy's not here."

The lady said "Children!" like she frustrated of me and she hanged up.

I lied the telephone down. It made noises. I put it back on its stand. The taste of the gum was finished. I throwed it into the wastebasket and chewed the other part. I wrote some more letters to Mommy and made some pictures. "Mommy, why you don't come? Please answer. In your own words. Are you hiding? Tell me."

I was bored of writing. I goed to the living room and climbed on the piano bench. I played and singed. "Old McDonald had a farm. E I E I 0. On this farm he keeped some cows. E I E I 0." That was no fun. I climbed down and went to my room for my bucket and shovel. "Wanna' build with me?" I said to Curious George, "It's very fun." Curious George didn't mind and I jumped up and down. "Wanna' play? Yes? Okay? Okay?"

Me and George went out one of the French doors. I filled the bucket with dirt and packed it. I needed wet dirt. I drinked some water from the hose and putted some in the bucket. I mixed the dirt and water and I packed it and turned it over and banged. I lifted carefully. Only one corner was crumbly. I'm good at castles. I put a twig on top for a flag. I made another castle and connected a road. I goed in to get a truck. The telephone ringed and I knocked over some things and runned. I was crying. I picked up the telephone. "Yes? Yes? Yes?"

A Man said. "Hi."

I said, "Hi."

Man said, "I sorry I had to leave in a hurry last night. I had important business. Today I come and take care of you."

He didn't sound nice. "Who you?" I said. "I want my Mommy."

"I know where your mommy is. Wait there for me. I'm coming."

SKIP

She was always saying, "Wait'll I tell your father." It was her favorite expression. They were the worst words in the whole world.

I said, "I didn't mean it. I'm sorry."

She said, "Don't tell me you're sorry. Tell your father."

I begged her but she wouldn't listen. "I promise I won't do it again," I said.

"He'll make sure of that," she said.

"Please, please, please."

She said to stop making so much noise and set the table. I could hardly hold the dishes because my hands were shaking so much. I thought I might drop a plate. That would make it worse. I said, "I'll be good if you don't tell him. I'll do anything you want. Wash dishes and take out the garbage."

"You'll do those things anyway," she said.

"I didn't know it was stealing," I said, "It was on a tree outside. Justin said it was okay."

"Now you're blaming your friend Justin," she said.

"No I'm not," I said. "I'm just telling you. It was outside. Not like inside a house or a store."

"You think it's all right to steal outside?" she said. "If I leave the car outside it's all right to steal it?"

"I'll be good. I'll do anything you say."

"I'm sure you will," she said.

I grabbed her around the legs. She said, "Stop that blubbering. You don't have anything to blubber about yet. Wait'll your father gets home. Then you'll have something to blubber about."

I ran to my bedroom and started to get in my pajamas. If he thought I was asleep maybe he wouldn't get me. It was too late. I heard the door open and him talking to Mother. I began biting my finger so hard it began to bleed.

"Where is he?" Father said.

"You know him," Mother said. "He's pretending to be asleep."

"It won't do him any good." I heard that funny sound in his voice. Not just

angry. That wasn't so bad. It was something worse.

"Come out this minute, Skip," he said. "I'm counting to ten."

I could hear his footsteps coming closer. It was so scary I couldn't stand it. When Father said, "Two," I ran out.

"I didn't mean it," I said. "I didn't know it was stealing to take grapes. I only had about three."

Father grabbed me. Mother stood in the doorway watching.

"First go down on your knees," Father said, "and ask for God's forgiveness. Then we'll take care of my forgiveness."

Then he started. I couldn't help it. I yelled and yelled but we were too far away from any neighbors for anybody to hear.

FIVE

Thursday, June 7
Faith

The next train to South Springport was at 12:05. The Downeaster.

I picked the shortest ticket line but the man at the head of the line was having a difference of opinion about credit cards with the ticket agent. His had apparently expired. I glanced at the big clock. 11:35.

"South Springport," I said when I finally reached the window. It was a man this time but with the same snarling face as the woman ticket agent. Apparently, working for Amtrak was not a fulfilling job and friendliness was not a job requirement.

"Twenty-two dollars."

I counted the bills and change in my fist. Impatient mutters filled the air behind me as I fumbled for my money. I was so nervous that I dropped a quarter and had to pursue it as it rolled away across the floor. Meanwhile, the line of people closed together and my place in line disappeared.

"Hey, it's my turn," I protested.

"Speed it up, Lady," the ticket agent growled, "These people have trains to catch."

As if I didn't. I cut back into the front of the line. He wouldn't have spoken to me that way if I'd looked like the woman behind me with her short black skirt, long blue jacket and even longer legs.

I had twelve dollars and fifty cents. That would teach me to be charitable.

"Lady, move aside while you find the fare," the ticket agent said.

I still had time. In any case, if I missed this train, there was always another.

No, I had to hurry.

I stopped a girl in a big tee shirt, tight shorts, jogging shoes and a backpack. "Please help me. I need money for my little boy."

My little boy? An out of control carousel whirled in my head, lights flashing, animals racing by in a blur, music blaring. It was going so fast I was sure all the little riders would be hurled, as if from a brightly colored centrifuge, to their deaths.

The girl spread her arms. "Sorry. I have just enough to get home."

I was out of earshot before she could finish speaking. Hurrying from person to person, I held out my hand, but everyone dodged around me. Back out on the street, a man gave me a leaflet urging me to have false nails pasted over my own. I dropped it into a trashcan quickly, afraid that the other side of the leaflet would reveal another missing child.

Five or six shoppers were gathered around an outdoor fruit stand, among them a well dressed middle-aged woman in a beige pants suit who had placed her tan shoulder bag on the edge of the cart while she selected peaches. With neither hesitation nor guilt, I picked up the purse and walked away. I kept expecting to hear an outcry behind me, but nothing happened as I crossed the street against a light, was nearly knocked over by a bicyclist who cursed at me, and reached the train station again.

In a cubicle in the women's room, I examined my acquisition. The purse was made of expensive leather, inside and out, and the smell of the leather reminded me of . . . something. For some reason, I immediately recognized that the brand was "Coach". Hidden in various compartments were keys, a hairbrush, a lipstick, a packet of tissues, a notepad, a pen, a train schedule, credit cards and a wallet. Exotic souvenirs from an alien planet. The wallet contained six twenties, a ten, a five and seven singles as well as change. I was awed by my plunder. Hastily, I extracted two twenties and returned to the station. 11:57.

I went to the head of the line. "Please, can you let me in? My train leaves in a few minutes."

Sharp objections. But an elderly man at the front of the line waved me ahead of him.

"Thank you." I wanted to hug him but could easily imagine him recoiling in horror if I attempted such a thing.

"South Springport, I'm trying to catch the 12:05." It was like throwing down the gauntlet. The ticket agent – the same one as a few minutes ago – stared at his computer terminal thoughtfully and then began typing. It seemed to me he typed a novella length document before a ticket finally emerged from the computer printer. I threw the twenty and the five on the counter, scooped up my ticket, and raced to the track. As I ran by, another trashcan caught my attention. Clearly the purse was an incongruous accessory to the rest of my outfit, but I couldn't force myself to part with it. Instead, I hid it between my arm and my body.

I raced out to the track and entered a car. I sat down behind two men discussing home improvements on their summer homes near York Beach. One was fat and homely and well dressed, the other slim, handsome and sloppily dressed in a sweatshirt and jeans. The fat one was pumping the slim one for advice about local carpenters, electricians and plumbers. The thin one was holding back from giving the information with the tenacity of someone who had trained during the Inquisition. I leaned forward. "How long does it take to get to Portland?"

"Two and a half hours." It was the fat one who answered.

"Are there many stops between Boston and Portland?"

"About seven." With some impatience this time.

I was starved. Why hadn't I stolen fruit along with the purse? No time to run back to one of the food stands. As soon as the train started I felt sleepy. Suppose I rode past my destination? I looked for the conductor but he was gone. My mind wandered off again. A memory, one I wasn't sure I wanted to recall, crossed my field of awareness and then wafted away. The clacking of the wheels was echoed by a clacking inside my head.

Without knowing what I was going to do, I took the notepad and pen from the purloined purse and began sketching. The interior of the train came into focus as if I were rubbing a chemical solution over invisible ink.

Something wrong about the sketch. The last time I had viewed this scene, it had been from a different angle.

SIX

Thursday, June 7
Dilly

In the olden days Mommy and me used to have treasure hunts in the crawl space. She hided presents and I finded them. She made hints. Like hot, cold, freezing.

I didn't like the Man on the telephone. He made me scared. Like the bad guy in Aladdin. Maybe the Man a magician. A beast even. I went to the basement, to the work room where my Dad builded things before he died in a car accident in California. New Jersey maybe. I was almost a baby. I pushed a box to the workbench and climbed up next to the drill press. It's okay to go near the drill press when no power. I climbed into the crawl space. I'm pretty much a good climber. Mommy and I climb rocks in 'Cadia. Also a pretend rock in the playground. I can climb the hardest rope in the playground. It swings when you climb.

I putted on the crawl space light. I looked for a place to hide. Mommy has to bend but I can stand straight. The light only reached part way but I can see even with no electricity because a crack in the back wall where sun comes in. The floor is concrete. The ceiling is the floor upstairs.

I forgetted why I here. I opened the scratched old trunk used to be my Daddy's grandfather. He died probably a hundred years ago. One time in a treasure hunt I finded a coloring pad and crayons there. I pretty much like to draw. But I like trucks better. Nothing in the trunk except some old curtains. Maybe Mommy hided new treasures before she went away. I looked. No treasures.

I'm too little to be alone. What aliens are? They eat people, right? Cindy says no but Chris says yes. Tracy doesn't know.

I sitted on the floor next to the dollhouse, used to be Mommy's when she a little girl. I pushed the tiny cradle. It rocked. The doll was big as my finger. I was careful because Mommy said we have to save the dollhouse in case I get a baby sister. I asked when. She didn't know. When you marry I said. She said yes. Who you marry I said. She said, you're a goose. I get a new Daddy I said. She said yes. I said will I like him. She laughed. You *love* him she said. It was Moore.

I lied on my stomach so I could see inside the dollhouse. Beds and kitchens and pictures. A lamp even. It didn't light like the one in the museum. I'm bored of museums. I go to them pretty much. I explored around in case I missed a treasure. I finded a big vanilla envelope with Mommy's papers from school. Why called vanilla? It tasted bad. Not vanilla. My old high chair from when I was little. We can take it upstairs when Mommy gets the new baby. A lot of dishes wrapped in newspapers. They're valuable. My old tricycle. I have a big one now in the garage. Also a John Deere tractor I can ride. It's too heavy for me to take out myself. A stuffed rabbit used to belong to Daddy when he was a kid. I hugged. "Wanna' kiss?" I said. Lots of Christmas ornaments. I unwrapped carefully. One was a wooden sleigh with Santa Claus. Last Christmas I heared Santa Claus' bell in the chimney. I was scared. But only a little bit. Some were sparkly.

Somebody knocked outside. What should I do? Answer? Could be Mommy. I heared that Man say, "Open this door. I've come to take care of you."

He didn't sound nice. Angry even. He could come in any door. Some always open. Should I hide? Maybe he was nice. Maybe he knowed where Mommy goed. More bangs. Then nothing. I was pretty afraid. The garage door opened. I made a sound. Like the mouse Mommy killed with the broom. I turned off the light in the crawl space. The Man goed upstairs. I heared sounds like doors and closets. The Man said, "You playing hide and seek? I know you here. Come out."

I can tell voices, I know pretending from real. He was pretending friendly.

Footsteps comed down. "You're making me annoyed," He said. "I can see through walls. I can see in the dark."

He sees through walls? In the dark? Monsters can see through walls. Was he teasing? I crawled back more. The footsteps were on the bottom. He went in the playroom. He said, "I can see you."

If he could see me, why he ask where am I? He fooling me. I hided in a dark corner. Behind the trunk. He was really mad.

"Are you in the basement?" he said. He called me a little creep. What's creep?

"You inside a wine bottle?" he said, "In the fireplace? You don't come out

I'll make a fire in the fireplace."

He mean it? I wasn't in the fireplace. Fire is danger. Mommy said never play with matches. I squished up tiny behind the trunk. A blanket there. I chewed it. It tasted awful. The Man was making noises. Mommy's skis fell to the floor. He crashed the old coffee table. He throwed something. Maybe the ping pong racket.

"What this?" the Man said. He opened the door to the workroom.

"A hiding place?" He putted his head into the opening of the crawl space. He said, "A secret room."

I was afraid. Very. I feeled like the time I putted my hand in the wall plug. It sizzled. The Man said, "Aha." He climbed in. I hided my head. I couldn't see. I bited the blanket. Christmas tree ornaments crunched. He didn't care. He broke Mommy's favorites, probably. Maybe the sleigh. I wondered he hear my heart?

"Could the little bugger go off in the woods?" the Man said. The voice was different. Not teasing. He went back out. I listened. The garage door banged.

It was a trick? He waiting behind the corner like Chris sometimes? Chris jumps and yells, "Got you!" I hate that.

I taked the blanket out of my mouth. It tasted terrible. Chris says he prays when he wants something. I don't know much prayers. What should I say? God, make Mommy come back? Would he?

I falled asleep.

SKIP

I went to the hospital for an appendix operation. It was the best time of my life. I wasn't afraid of anybody and the food was delicious. Nobody was ever angry. The first day when I woke up the nurse asked me if I was thirsty. I said yes and she brought me lemonade. There were little drops of condensed water on the outside of the glass. The nurse was fat and she had rough skin but I loved her.

The boy in the next bed had a lot of toys and he lent me a coloring book and crayons. I liked the coloring book but I like empty pages best where I can draw my own pictures. Mother says I'm weird. The boy had a hundred visitors. Lots of relatives. I didn't have anybody except Mother and Father. The boy's mother was sorry for me, I could tell. She was always giving me things. I told her I had lots of toys at home. A train set with tracks and toy soldiers. She said, "You ought to ask your mother to bring you some." I told her they were Father's when he was young. They were too valuable for the hospital. She gave me clay and a book called Grimm's Fairy Tales. I said, "For keeps?" and she said yes. She read us stories. One was called Charlotte's Web.

The nurse said, "Good news. Your mother is coming to take you home." I thought my heart would stop. I wanted to stay in the hospital forever.

I said, "I'm not better." She said, "Appendicitis is not very serious." She looked funny. She said, "Don't you want to go home?" I said I ought to stay for another day because I wasn't all better yet. She said the scar would hurt for a few days but that was all. She said, "Once you're home, you can lie in bed. Play. Read. Have fun."

What did she know?

I tried not to cry but I cried anyway. I was afraid she'd tell Father. She went away and came back with the doctor. He sat on the bed and asked why I was crying. I said I didn't know. He asked about the marks on my body and I said, "I fall a lot. I'm very careless."

The day Father and Mother came to take me home, the fat nurse wasn't there. I wanted to see her but it was her day off.

She told the new nurse to give me a hug and a kiss.

Mother and Father came to get me and Father said, "Well, Son, time to go home." He never called me son when we were alone. Only in front of people. He had that nice happy laughing voice for when other people were around.

The doctor said, "He seems upset about leaving the hospital."

I yelled, "I'm not upset! I want to leave!"

Father said, "Take it easy Son," and he touched my head and smiled. I hate his smile. The ends of his mouth go up but he gets lines between his eyes. Mother and Father and the doctor went in the hall and I could hear them talking but not the words. I sat up and listened hard. I heard Father say, "He's the clumsiest kid in the world. He's always falling down stairs or off his bike."

The boy in the next bed said, "You told me you don't have a bike."

I didn't answer.

"You can have one of my bikes," he said.

"You giving me a bike?" I said.

"Just for a while. Until my cousin grows into it."

I wished I had a cousin. I said, "Your mother will let you do that?"

"My mother was the one told me to do it," he said.

Mother, Father and the doctor came back.

"Time to get up lazy bones," Father said. He sounded like other fathers. Maybe he was going to change. I got out of bed and went to the bathroom to put on my clothes. I could hear a lot of sounds through the door. Like somebody calling for a doctor over the loud speaker and the wheels of the food carts. I was going to miss the sounds.

The doctor left and Father saw all the stuff the kid's mother had given me. "Where did you get this?" he said. I told him.

"Time to give it back," he said.

"His mom said I could keep it," I said. The kid called his mother mom.

"Your mother told Skip he could keep all this?" Father said to the kid.

"Yes," the kid said. "Also I'm going to lend him my bike."

"He has his own bike," Father said.

"No, he doesn't," the kid said.

Father laughed. "He's fooling you," he said. He put the toys back on the other kid's bed.

Father said, "Thank you for lending Skip your things."

"I gave them to him," the kid said.

"He has too many of his own things at home," Father said.

I wanted to yell, "No, I don't," but I kept quiet. Father gripped my hand so hard it almost made me cry.

"Say goodbye to your friend," he said.

"Goodbye," I said.

I knew I was bad because I'd acted like I didn't want to go home. Also because

I took presents from the kid and told him I didn't have a bike. Father wasn't going to change. I wanted to ask the nurse and the doctor and the lady behind the desk to help me but I knew they wouldn't.

SEVEN

Thursday, June 7
Faith

The Portland station was both familiar and unfamiliar, not as I had pictured it in my mental album, but not completely strange either.

Was this the right station stop?

The other passengers disembarking from the train darted quick glances at me before averting their eyes. They were wearing business suits or the type of sportswear I somehow knew came from catalogs.

I walked out the station door to the street. I thought about taking a bus but before I could figure that out, I saw a cab. A gray haired man with a roll of flesh hanging over his belt was leaning against the car. He opened his mouth to ask if I needed a ride and then took a second look and changed his mind.

"Could you tell me," I asked him, "when did they build that store across from the station?" I pointed to it.

He glanced behind him.

He thought a moment and then shrugged, "Maybe eight, nine years ago."

Was he lying? Deranged? Had a sorcerer reconstructed the station surroundings overnight? What year had that man at the shelter said it was? I couldn't remember.

Now what?

"Could you give me a ride?"

"Where to?"

Home.

Home? The word slid around inside my skull like a pinball slipping along the slanted surface, unable to find a stationary perch. Home was a park bench. A grate over steam heat. A storefront. A shelter.

"Freeport." I didn't think Freeport was my home but I knew he wouldn't think I was insane if I gave that name.

"It's thirty bucks to Freeport," he said, glancing back down at my outfit. "Maybe you want to take the bus. You can get one back in the station."

I thought about it but decided to splurge. If I was on a bus, I couldn't ask the driver to stop just anywhere on the way.

"I think I'll take a cab."

He didn't move. I realized that he didn't think I had the resources to splurge.

I opened the magic purse, pulled out a nice black leather wallet, opened it and rifled through the cash as if to confirm that I had sufficient funds, although I knew full well that I did.

It was like magic. He pushed himself away from where he had been leaning on the cab, opened the back door and waved me in.

We drove out of Portland and drove North on Route 295. For about ten miles, I simply stared out the window, half recognizing some of the landscape but not all. It was like looking at an historical photograph and recognizing a building here or there but not the rest of the scene.

As we approached Freeport, I suddenly sat forward and nearly yelling, said, "Take the next exit. The South Springport exit."

Without commenting, the driver veered off the highway onto the exit. At the bottom of the ramp, he didn't even bother to ask but just stopped the car.

"Go right please. Into South Springport."

He nodded and in a couple of miles we were there.

I knew it was the right town. A small town that looked as if it might have gone from being a New England town where prosperous merchants and sea captains lived to a dying New England artifact. And now, most recently, it was enjoying a Renaissance born of tourism and suburban sprawl.

"I'll get out here," I said and handed him thirty dollars. Only after he had driven away did it occur to me that the fare should have been under thirty dollars since we had not gone as far as Freeport but, limited as my resources were, I didn't care.

Beyond the compact group of stores that formed the commercial center of the town, there were big white houses set close to the main street, relics of the days when the richest inhabitants built in the vicinity of the village church. I arbitrarily started walking east. A little further on, I passed an elementary school surrounded by playing fields, a small granite stone church, and then small plots of land with modest ranch houses representing the town's less prosperous period during the 1940's and 1950's. Soon the fields and woods took over and now the dwellings were either ancient restored farmhouses built next to the road, or else invisible structures approached by long wooded driveways.

What was I doing? I was following my nose, but who knew if my nose was a trustworthy leader or a false prophet beckoning me towards nowhere on a road towards nothing?

About a mile out of town, I began to wonder about where I would sleep. In the city there were boundless possibilities, but the country had no park benches or shelters. Long ago, hobos – there were no "homeless" then – slept in barns. Kindly farmers' wives provided them with food in return for fence repairs. What did I know about fence repairs? Besides which, there didn't seem to be an over abundance of authentic farms or kindly farmers' wives in the area.

Water Wheel Road. Maybe it touched off a ping of memory. Or maybe it was the siren song of the crickets that sounded familiar. Or perhaps the split rail fence that fronted an old gray barn bathed by the afternoon sun in a pink glow. In any case, I turned into the narrow paved road.

A pile of newspapers in a blue plastic envelope lying at the end of a driveway brought me to a halt. Obviously, the owner was out of town and had forgotten to suspend his subscription. An open invitation to thieves like me.

Voices from the past: "When opportunity knocks, jump." "But how does one recognize opportunity?" "One can't. So keep jumping."

A low stonewall fronted by day lilies and hostas meandered across the front of the property. I walked down the front walk between a row of crab apple trees to a neat, small white clapboard house which had begun life as a farmhouse but had since been gentrified. Behind the house I could see a meadow with more flowering apple and cherry trees. I walked up two steps, flanked by large lead planters filled with geraniums, onto the porch. The front mullioned windows on either side of the front door were full length. I could have seen inside if they hadn't been shielded by cream-colored curtains. Although the place had a deserted air, I knocked on the front door and waited. Nobody home. I glanced behind me. I was at least partially shielded from the road by the trees in the front yard.

I walked around to the side of the house. There was another small porch with a slate terrace floor that led up to a side door. Locked. In back was a large flagstone terrace furnished with a wrought iron table, teak chairs, chaise lounge and loveseat. Although it had not been visible from the road, now that I was behind the house, I saw that there was a pond about twenty feet back from the terrace, surrounded by purple irises in full bloom. (Since when had I become such a botanical expert?) A back door that opened from the terrace into a dining room was also locked. Beyond the pond was the meadow and beyond that, a thickly wooded steep hill.

The barn. My accommodations for the night. The barn stood a few hundred feet away from the house. I crossed the lawn and found my first unlocked door. This had once been a working barn. I was standing in what looked like a milking shed for ten or twelve cows. It had not yet been gentrified, although one could easily imagine that within a generation, this would be, in the words of some future realtor, a charming in-law apartment. Neatly stacked on a long wooden bench were cans, brushes, pots, paint remover, mixing sticks and turpentine. Wrenches, screwdrivers, pliers, and hammers were arranged on a pegboard. Larger tools: rakes, shovels, axes and gardening tools, were hung neatly on wrought iron hooks along the back wall. Very tidy owners. Enthusiastic hobbyists.

Through a door on my right, was the large central portion of the barn with a hayloft that gave off the musty smell of old hay. Massive hand hewn beams crisscrossed from side to side. Some day those beams would be tastefully exposed below the high then-to-be sky-lighted ceilings.

As a shelter it wasn't much of an improvement over a park bench – nothing to lie on, no coverings for warmth. But the principle drawback was the lack of food. Now that I was rich, why hadn't I bought something in town? Well, for one thing, I hadn't noticed a grocery market. For another, I'd been preoccupied. In any case, I was too tired to go back.

The hell with it. With no more hesitation than when I'd snatched the purse, I picked up a pair of gardening shears and gloves and returned to the house. I chose a back mullioned window next to the back dining room door in case anyone passed by on the road. I cut out the screen. Then, standing to one side, I smashed the glass in one pane with the shears. I gingerly reached through the window and opened the dining room door.

I was in a small dining room with an oval cherry wood table, six wooden dining chairs, and a small matching sideboard. The dining room led to the front hall and from there to a narrow kitchen. In the living room, two flowered sofas flanked the fireplace, and between them, a wooden chest served as a coffee table. The walls were lined with books. I didn't bother to look at the titles. All of the furnishings, except for the sofas and books, seemed to be genuine antiques. (Although how would I know?) There was a small bedroom off of the living room with a four-poster bed, white coverlet, and a small oriental rug on the floor. A small bathroom off of this bedroom had an old-fashioned claw footed tub.

Everything was neat and tasteful but unused looking. It was a lovely scene. A house that would have stood up well in a book with a name like *Country Living* or *New England Style*. But why was I wasting time inventorying the house when I needed to get on with it?

And most of all, what was the "it" I needed to get on with?

First things first. I found a broom closet in the kitchen and swept up the broken glass. You would have to look carefully to notice that the small pane was gone. I went back to the barn to return the shears and hide the broken glass in a bucket. I returned to the kitchen. The refrigerator, like the rest of the house, had a great deal of clean empty space, but the white kitchen cabinets held cans of soup and tuna fish, spaghetti, cereals, sauces, spices, flour, and sugar. In the freezer were frozen loaves of bread, a frozen steak and vanilla ice cream. I put one of the frozen loaves of bread in the oven to defrost and opened a can of tomato soup and tuna fish. While the soup warmed, I ate the tuna fish with my fingers from the can. When the bread was ready, I cut off three slices and ate them with the soup.

Behaving as if I were an obsessive housewife who had lived here always, I cleaned up afterwards, just as I had cleaned up the broken glass. Why? To hide the evidence of my presence? Or to appease the spirit of this pristine house? I felt as if I were engaged in some half remembered routine. Something like riding a bicycle I supposed. I had once lived in a house. Not this house, but a house like this. A house with curtains and rugs and pretty country views.

At this point, I was so exhausted from my trip and these activities that I needed a breather. Taking off the scuffed brown boots, I stretched out on the living room sofa and propped a blue silk pillow under my head. I was suddenly filled with a wonderful calm, as if this business of lying on a sofa in a lovely clean room filled with antiques and books was where I belonged. It almost felt as if I deserved to be there.

But then I recalled that I had started out the day homeless on a park bench. I began to map out a plan. First, I would return to the village and check into all the stores to see if anyone recognized me. If no one did, I would walk up and down the roads until I started to see houses that seemed familiar. My eyes closed.

For an instant when I woke up I thought I might be back in the shelter. But I felt too comfortable and the air smelled better. No gas fumes. No garbage cans banging against each other or blaring sirens.

For a few minutes I stared, half aware of my surroundings, at a dark gray rectangle. Then I realized that it was a window and jumped to my feet. It was nearly dark outside. All the stores would be closed and all the houses too dark to see. I had lost an entire day. The fact that I didn't know what I had lost if *from* didn't help. I swayed back and forth, holding my aching head in my hands. There was still enough light for me to find my way to the downstairs bathroom. I turned on the light and opened the medicine cabinet – clean and empty except for soap and Motrin. I swallowed three Motrin pills and then froze.

A light had been switched on in the living room. Why should I be surprised? Why should I have assumed that no one would come home to this house? Perhaps because it had seemed so neat and uninhabited.

Through the open door of the bathroom I had a view of a corner of the sofa, a side table and a green ceramic lamp with an ivory shade. The light was on but no one was standing next to it. Then, while I stood there, another lamp silently went on.

Automatic switches to foil burglars. But not a burglar like me.

It made no sense to leave the house now. I would have to wait until morning. Somehow, I had a renewed confidence that no one would be coming home that night. But what if they did? I needed a warning system. Something like . . . a trip wire, although I wasn't even sure what that was. In any event, it was too complicated for a spongy mind like mine.

The immaculate house suddenly made me feel unclean, more so than usual. I removed the rusty black jacket, the yellowed blouse, the black skirt and graying underwear and put them in the washing machine. I knew all about washing machines. Nothing strange about that; most shelters had them.

Next I went back to the bathroom and turned on the faucets. While waiting for the claw-footed tub to fill, I examined myself in the small mirror. My face glided in and out of focus. My thoughts scattered into different cracks and crevices around my brain, preventing me from making any further connections.

When the tub was full, I eased myself in and allowed my head to sink under the surface as if to shed my outer skin. I knew it had been a long time since I had had a shower and much, much longer since I had lain in a bathtub. Mist rose from the steaming water and my limbs floated languidly, my hair streamed away from my head like seaweed. It was even more wonderfully familiar than lying on the sofa. I found some soap and shampoo and scrubbed myself. Then I rinsed off and wrapped a large blue, clean – wonderfully clean – towel around me. I changed my laundry from the washer to the dryer and went up the narrow staircase to examine the second floor. Was I considering making an offer?

On my right was a low ceilinged room with twin beds and a tall old-fashioned chest of drawers. On the left was a larger room with a big four-poster bed, a brocade coverlet, polished oak flooring, and a love seat that matched the coverlet. A long narrow hallway, flanked by closets and built in drawers, led to another bathroom. Beyond that, there was a tiny room with an oval window that looked out towards the barn. There was room here only for a small daybed and an armchair. It looked as if it might have been planned for a child who had failed to come off the drawing board.

I closed the door gently (so as not to disturb the ghost-child?) and went back along the corridor, opening closets and drawers. Men's suits, shoes, shirts, underwear, socks, sweaters, slacks. No sign of a woman.

I went back down the stairs to the first floor, and still waiting for my clothes to dry, examined the address notebook beside the telephone on the kitchen counter. None of the names evoked a response.

A photograph beside the telephone, held in a painted wooden frame, showed two dark haired Hispanic looking children.

I opened the desk. Bills and letters addressed to Guy North.

A piggy bank on one of the bookshelves that flanked the fireplace held nickels, dimes, quarters and half dollars. For a moment I felt as if I'd found a treasure chest, enough to keep me in luxury for months. Experimentally, I turned it over but nothing fell out. I decided not to break it. My unwitting host had done enough for me. Besides, I had my other treasure, the stolen purse.

My clothes were made of synthetic fabrics and dried quickly. I dressed but didn't know what to do next. I stood indecisively in the downstairs bedroom, looking out towards the pond. A half moon was coming up. A hood of desolation slid over my head as if I were being readied for hanging.

The house had been lying in wait for me. Like the beast for Beauty, the witch for Gretel, the bears for Goldilocks. But since I was no Beauty, no Gretel, no Goldilocks, the story's ending could not be predicted.

The flowers were no longer visible, the terrace could have been a large black pit and the pond, so lovely a few hours before, had transmogrified itself into a slimy black swamp, a stage setting for a scene in a horror movie.

EIGHT

Thursday, June 7
Dilly

I waked and saw the crack where light comed in. That's how I knowed I was in the crawl space. How many days I alone? I don't like this. I don't want to grow up. I don't want to be big. I don't want to be dead. What are those guys who live with God? Angels. What they look like? They mostly dead?

Mommy, why you not come? I listened. Nothing. No creaks, no footsteps. No opening doors. No sound of talking. I goed to the hole and crawled out to the worktable to the floor. I goed up the stairs.

I holded the banister and listened. Mommy says always hold banister. I looked through between the door and the wall. No Man. I goed to the kitchen. It was a huge mess. Mommy wouldn't like it. Juice on the floor, food all over. I'm too little to clean. I dragged the stool to the counter and wished I could fill my bottle. But I'm too big for a bottle. I drinked from a glass and was very careful. No spilling. I eated a banana. I was tired of bananas. Don't eat too fast. You get a stomach ache.

Was Mommy talking to me? I looked but no luck. I broke a piece of bread.

If the Man comed back, he know I here because bread missing? Also a banana? I stuffed the bread in back of the cabinet. That way Man wouldn't see I eated it.

I goed to my room and readed my book. Big storm in the book. Big big storm, I putted out my hands to show Curious George. Also bad fog. Horn goes hoo, hoo. The picture had a big rock and kids diving. Also a rowboat and a rubber raft. Mommy taked me to the beach a lot in the olden days. We found beautiful rocks. Also shells. I goed to the bathroom and pooped and the telephone ringed.

Mommy says the telephone always ringed when she's in the bathroom.

I got stuck in my shorts and stuff when I runned to the telephone. Maybe the Man checking? Maybe Mommy? I pushed the stool to the telephone. Only a dial tone. I hanged up and goed to the bathroom to finish pooping.

I looked out the window. What time of day it is? I don't know. What day? Today or yesterday? I goed to Mommy's room and pushed the button on the remote control. Numbers like a puzzle and three people talking and laughing. It wasn't interesting. Why laughing? I clicked off and goed to my room and putted on my fireman boots. Never go out alone, Mommy's voice said, but it wasn't really Mommy. I won't go near the pool, I said inside my head. Mommy says if something happens, go to Mrs. B. I taked my pail and shovel and also Curious George. I couldn't take Blanky. Too much things to carry. I yelled, "Race you," and runned down the driveway. It was a long way. On the road I heared a car and I hided behind the stonewall. I was glad I hided. It was the Man. He drived up the driveway. He looking for me? Why?

I don't like him. I stayed close to the woods in case he comed down the driveway again. Sometimes when Mommy and I go to Mrs. B. Mommy carries me part way. Sometimes even she pushes the stroller. I'm actually too big for the stroller but I get tired a lot. How long it take to get to Mrs. B.? I forgot. Two hours maybe.

Mrs. B. is nice. I love her. She hugs a lot. She gives me ice cream. I don't tell Mommy. It's our secret. Mommy says ice cream makes cavities. Another car, not the Man's. I runned out but the guy didn't see me. I tried to run up the hill but George too heavy. I rested on a rock. Mrs. B. have a bottle for me? No way, Jose. Mrs. B. doesn't have her own kids.

Mommy say all the time, "Stay to the left." Where's left? She say, "Watch out for cars." No cars. I saw litter. A beer can and a McDonald box. Maybe French fries. No luck. Mommy says bad people litter. I throwed the box and the can in the woods. It wasn't far enough. I could still see. I decided I'd cut short to Mrs. B. in the woods. Sometimes Mommy and I did that. I went in the woods. Branches hitted me. I finded a stick to help me walk. On top of the hill I tried to see Mrs. B.'s house. Too far. I got afraid. Maybe I wouldn't find it. I stopped to rest and look at things. There were Jacks in Pulpit. Mommy told me the name. I help a lot in the garden. I have a garden belongs to me. With sunflower seeds.

I seed Mrs. B's house and runned. She'd probably give me lemonade. Soda even. A car came so fast I couldn't even hide. A lady said, "Get off the road, Little Boy. Somebody ought to tell your mother."

I watched the lady drive away.

"Get ready, get set, go!" I runned and George falled. I throwed the stick so I could hold George better. I zigzagged. The house wasn't a mirage. A mirage is when you see it even if not there. It's like 'magination.

Mrs. B. is a very good gardener. She has a million flowers. I forget the names. I sniffed. No smell. I knocked on the door but no answer. Usually I'm polite but I began to bang. I banged hard. I kicked the door with my boot and yelled, "Mrs. B., please!" She didn't answer. I found a big rock and throwed it at the wall. It made a mark. I didn't care. I wasn't even sorry. I yelled, "Mrs. B., come out!" She didn't.

I had a tantrum but nobody seed. I picked up a chair folded close to the house. It was 'luminum. I climbed and ringed the bell. I could hear ringing. Tears comed into my mouth and I wanted a bottle. I didn't know what to do. I was too tired to go home. I sitted in the garden. I digged and filled my pail. The dirt made good castles. When the pail was filled, I turned it upside down carefully and banged with the shovel. I picked up the pail. It was a good castle. Only a little crumbly on one side. I builded two castles. I made a road in between. A flower falled by mistake. I tried making it stand. It didn't. Actually it was worser.

I couldn't see because night time coming. I didn't cry. I picked up my pail and shovel and George and goed to the garage. There was a door I could open. No car. No food. I looked at the garden. No vegetables. Never put things in your mouth unless I tell you, Mommy said. She was talking inside me again. I liked it. She was watching, even though I didn't see her. "Not even apple?" I said. She called me a little goose.

I holded up my fingers. That's how long Mommy away. Before she always told me when she goed away. Cindy baby sitted me. Mommy leaved presents and called always. Now no Cindy. No presents. "Don't be a baby," Mommy said. "I always come back, Snoogums. We're a team." I finded a burlap bag in the garage and I lied down. George made me company. I wished I had Blanky. Also my bottle. I don't care if bottles are for babies. I was tired from the walk. I sleeped.

SKIP

It was so dark I thought I was blind. Not dark like in the night when you can see the window but black. I opened my mouth to yell but then I choked it back. It could be a trick. Father could be close by to catch me making a scene. I could hardly breathe. Also I had a lump in my throat like I swallowed something too big to go down. Where was I? How long had I been here? Could I ever get out? Maybe this was a dungeon. If I moved I might touch a snake, or fall down a hundred foot well and never get out. Maybe that's what happened. I could be here until I died and went to Hell and burned forever. I put my hands in my mouth so nobody could hear me crying. Maybe nobody was around to hear. If they didn't hear me, how could they rescue me? I was thirsty like the time Father put rags in my mouth.

I hurt all over. Did I faint? I faint a lot. Mother says I'm apt to go into a spell any time. I say strange things.

I saw a TV show once at somebody's house about a kid that fell in a well. She spent days there before she died. I reached out. I could feel wood. I wasn't in a dungeon. It was too small. I tried to pick up my head but it hit wood. I tried to hear, but I couldn't hear anything. I was lying on something scratchy like a blanket. I pushed against the sides but nothing budged. Then I knew where I was. I was in a coffin! I was buried alive!

Did Father make a mistake and think I was dead? Or was this a punishment? There was a ton of dirt on top of the coffin and I could never move it even if I got the coffin open. How much air was there? How long would it be before I used it all up? Mother always said how easy life would be if she didn't have me.

I couldn't help yelling. Anything was better than being buried alive. Even Father.

I heard Mother's voice. I nearly fainted again with relief. "Stop that racket!" she said. She sounded close. Was she buried too? Perhaps Father buried both of us. "Stop this minute," she said, "or I won't let you out."

I pushed my face in the scratchy stuff. I heard a bunch of bangs. Then the coffin opened. The sun made my eyes water. I was so happy I didn't ask how she got the dirt off so quickly.

I was in Mother's and Father's room. I was in the blanket chest! I couldn't understand why I couldn't open it from underneath. Then I saw the stack of books on the floor. Heavy books like the encyclopedia and dictionary had been piled on top of the chest before she took them off.

"I want to hear your apology," she said.

I apologized but I didn't know what I was apologizing about.

"You're lucky your father isn't here. If he heard that racket you were making you'd be back in there for the next twenty-four hours. Pick up the books and put them where they belong."

"Can I have a drink first?"

"The books first."

I did what she said and drank two glasses of water. I stayed out of the way and didn't say anything when Father came home. I thought if I stayed out of the way and didn't say anything he wouldn't get mad. But usually he found something to get mad about anyway.

NINE

Friday, June 8
Faith

I had just turned off Water Wheel Road to Route 120 when a minivan pulled up beside me and a woman's voice called out, "Want a lift?"

She pushed back a sliding door and I climbed up on a high seat beside her. She was in her thirties, had an artfully cut head of curly blond hair and wore a black tee shirt, a short skirt of chino material and Espadrilles. Somehow I knew they were Espadrilles. It was as if I had come back to the country of my birth and I was recalling a long forgotten native language.

On the back seat were two little girls of about four and six, more or less copies of the woman. It was so . . . banal that I felt as if I had stepped into a movie scene, a scene that I might have watched on TV at a shelter.

"Going to town?" She tried not to stare at *my* clothing. Her skin was dry and there were little lines at the corners of her eyes from squinting into the sun, the same sun that had given her the gorgeous tan.

"Yes please, but you can drop me off anywhere if you're not going that far."

"No problem. It's where I'm headed."

As we drove along, I kept examining the countryside so as not to miss a landmark which might break up the fog in my head and allow the light to shine through. I had awakened that morning to the croaking of frogs instead of the clanging of garbage cans. And instead of finding myself on a bench, I had been lying on a luxurious mattress between clean sheets (with no hidden peas) in a spotless bedroom. Since I had slept in my clothes, all I had to do was brush my teeth with a new boxed brush I had found in the downstairs bedroom, comb my hair and, pocketing a twenty dollar bill, set out to seek my fortune.

Why couldn't I rid myself of fairy tale jargon? It was as if I'd regressed into childhood.

"Going to market?"

To market, to market to buy a fat pig. Perhaps it wasn't my own childhood I had regressed to, but someone else's. Tightening my loose thoughts, I said, "Yes." It sounded too abrupt so I added, "Actually I have a number of errands to run. You know." I didn't.

"How are you getting back?"

" I'd planned on walking both ways. I need the exercise. But when you offered me a ride, well – "

"Mommy," said a voice from the rear, "Can we get bubble gum?"

"My little boy always used to ask for bubble gum." The words welled up from an unknown source, bringing bile with them. If my stomach hadn't been empty, I'd have thrown up. I closed my eyes.

"I told you," the woman was saying, "no bubble gum. You're only nagging because you think I'll say yes with a stranger around." Her eyes shifted from the rear view mirror to me. "Your little boy?"

To ease my throbbing head, I leaned back against the seat.

"Do you have a headache? Here, have an aspirin." Like someone well acquainted with headaches and well supplied to combat them, she rummaged with her right hand in a leather trimmed straw bag on the console beside her and shook out wallet, eyeglass case, and paper clips before she came to a small flat tin of aspirins.

"Mommy, just one piece of bubble gum."

I took two aspirins and put them in a pocket for when I would have access to water.

"That does it! You can't have Amanda over today!" Then, apparently unable to switch to an adult tone on the fly, she snapped at me as if I were another errant child, "Where do you want to be dropped off?"

"Right here will be fine." The little girl began to wail and I had a nearly irresistible desire to tell her mother that she would be sorry one day, that she would wish she'd been more patient, that she would long to be given a chance to do it over again. That her child would be gone soon enough. One way or another.

"Thank you," I said. I closed the car door and waved but no one waved back. From the way the car veered erratically, I guessed that another argument had broken out.

The village glowed with the luminescence of familiarity. Controlled by a remote device in the hand of a higher being, I headed for the post office. A man held the door for me. When had that ever happened in the city? On my left were rows of letter boxes and on my right, raised counters where two people were sorting their mail, assigning junk to a rubbish bin and retaining an infinitesimal portion of their correspondence.

I went past the inner door and waited for the overweight, mousy looking clerk to recognize me. She didn't.

"Uh, two stamps, please." I handed her the twenty and she exchanged it for pictures of Olympic athletes and nineteen dollars and twenty-two cents. Had she made a mistake or had something happened to the price of stamps?

"Do I know you?" a voice asked from behind me.

My reaction was more fear than gratification. If this was what I had come to South Springport for, why was I sick with apprehension? I teetered between fleeing or turning to see who had asked the question. I turned.

The woman's appearance was worse than mine. She was wearing a worn flowered cotton house dress, a heavy old wool sweater and a disreputable wool hat.

"Yes," I said, "how are you?" Then I took a second look. In the heavy featured, pitted face, the eyes were like the blank boarded up windows of city tenements and I knew I had no basis for either fear or gratification. In a high, keening voice, she began calling, "Jeff! Jeff! Where are you?"

I watched a forlorn man steer the woman out of the post office and into a blue Oldsmobile. I wondered what his reaction would have been if I'd asked, "Do you know *me*?" Probably: "Oh God! Not another one!"

Standing irresolutely at the edge of the curb, I seemed to be receiving signals as if from an intermittent revolving beacon of a lighthouse. Warning me off or protecting me from the shoals?

The library beckoned. It was a neat colonial fronted by a trim garden; either a two hundred year old genuine article or a convincing facsimile. Children's room on the right, adult room to the left, and traditional central staircase leading to the reference stacks. Untraditional was the librarian: young, attractive and chic.

I positioned myself so that she could get a clear view of me. "May I borrow a book even if I don't own a library card?" I waited for her to exclaim, "Faith! Where have you been? Glad to have you back." Instead, glancing up from a computer screen she had been studying with a dazed expression, she said, "Pardon me?" No sign of recognition.

"May I borrow a book if I don't have a card?"

"Do you live in town?"

"Yes."

"Sure, browse away and when you have something, I'll ask you to fill out a card."

I turned to the shelves. Austen, Bronte, Conrad, Doyle. Familiar territory. But who were Zadie Smith and Khaled Hosseini? I chose *Emma* and bent over to fill out the card. Faith uh, Smith was too obvious. How about Wheelwright from Water Wheel Road?

But when it came to the address, without thinking, I wrote Salmon Kill Road. I stared. It was as if a Ouija board had pointed out the letters. And it wasn't as if Salmon Kill was an ordinary street name like Elm or Oak.

"Do you know Salmon Kill Road?" I asked the librarian.

Still wrapped up in demystifying her computer, she said, "What? Oh. Salmon Kill. No, I don't. Why?"

"I was just – have you lived in town long?"

"Four years. A rank newcomer. But even if I were living here fifty," – a patent impossibility since she was about thirty – "I wouldn't know all the roads. New ones crop up all the time. A contractor puts up a few houses for spec and names the road for his wife. You know. Kay Lane. Besides which, South Springport isn't only the name of the village. It's the name of the township."

"Oh God. You mean South Springport could include, well, all the surrounding villages?"

She was beginning to transfer her attention from the computer to me. Taking a closer look, she examined first my clothes and then my face. "Only Lambert Hill, Bald Point and Barrett Landing." Hastily, as if to reassure me, she added, "But mostly when people say South Springport they mean the village of South Springport. You know, what with most of the local stores being here and everything."

Back on the street, I waited for signals again. Second Time Around was an antique shop that I knew had once been a child's paradise – a tiny space crammed with Japanese-made puppets, mechanical ducks, puzzles, games, picture books and penny candies. (Where have all the children gone?) The Clip Joint: a hairdressing establishment where a girl with a long peasant outfit was blowing a customer's hair in every direction. (No ping of memory.) A realtor's office advertising a rambling Georgian on nine acres featuring six bedrooms – excluding servants' quarters – living room, library, study, den, playroom, kitchen, butler's pantry, pool, tennis court, stables. Five thousand a week rental. (Where did the owners of the five thousand a week rental go to have fun?) I passed a small restaurant with a counter and about ten tables. It was called the Familiar Drummer, although it wasn't to me. I realized I was hungry and went in. Inside there were two other customers, men in working clothes, and it struck me that, aside from the elderly caretaker husband of the

THE FLY MAN MURDERS

Alzheimer victim, these were the only men I had noticed all morning. Evidently South Springport was in a time warp where women did women's work and the men commuted to the real world to do whatever was left of men's work.

I sat at a table for ten minutes while the girl at the counter exchanged pleasantries with the two men on stools. I was beginning to feel invisible again, unable to make the transition from purgatory to beyond, when the girl finally wrenched herself away.

With the air of doing me a special favor, she asked, "What will it be?" No recognition.

"Grilled cheese and a chocolate milkshake."

"At this time of the morning?" She couldn't have sounded more disgusted if I'd ordered grilled slugs with a side of Anthrax.

"Okay, " I said in an effort to appease her, "Scrambled eggs, bacon, toast and coffee." Not mollified, she did the usual inspection of my clothing, shrugged, and disappeared. Another ten minutes ticked by (although not on any wrist watch of mine) before she returned. While I ate, I mentally chewed what the librarian had told me. It didn't matter that the *township* was South Springport. What had brought me here was the tiny village. All I had to do was find the road I had written on the library card. What road? The name was buried under a weight of inconsequential detail. Could I go back and ask the librarian what I had written? Tell her I had forgotten my own address? It wouldn't be long before the citizens of South Springport began to whisper about the oddly dressed stranger who roamed the streets, peering into stores and houses and asking odd questions.

I finished breakfast, paid the bill, leaving a generous tip in the undoubtedly futile hope that that might mellow the girl's nature, and walked back out into the bright sunshine.

Ebullience was the name of the gift shop. South Springport was heavy on cuteness. Without knowing why, I went inside. It was littered with objects one bought for others, not oneself: sachets, candle sticks, table mats, cloth napkins, guest towels, soaps, bits of china, silver and crystal, boxes of stationery with subtly colored flowers and birds printed on them, pot holders, frilly baby clothes, pillows decorated with sentiments on the order of "The older the violin, the sweeter the music." It was cheerful, clean and smelled of jasmine. Everything in the shop was bizarrely expensive.

"This is where I bought Edith a set of tablemats when she moved into her new house."

Had I said the words aloud or to myself? They remained in the atmosphere like vapor trailed from an airplane. But there was only the name, no features to go with it.

"Do you know a woman called Edith?" I asked the young woman behind the counter.

The girl's expression told me I was crossing the boundary from oddness to downright peculiarity. "Edith? Edith who?"

"She lives in town. I'm sure she's a customer of yours."

"I never knew *anybody* called Edith," she said with the finality of someone probably named Samantha. Or Stacy. Or Trish.

Now what? I walked out and stood on the green while a cab pulled up to the curb and discharged a black woman with tight black curls, a flowered blouse and a shapeless black skirt. A white woman with elaborately coiffed hair, gold hoop earrings and a pale silk blouse sat in a Mercedes waiting for her. The black woman got into the Mercedes and the white woman drove off with her housekeeper or nanny.

Would I recognize Edith if I saw her? I couldn't canvas the town asking women their first names. The local telephone book? In a town like South Springport, in most cases, only husbands' names would be listed. The church bulletin? That would probably list the first names of husbands *and* wives. (How did I know *that?*)

But the beautiful white steepled Presbyterian Church exuded no aura of familiarity, and I continued past, taking a new route out of town, this time going west on Route 170.

Less than a mile out of the village I came upon it.

Edith's house. It was set back from the road on a slight rise. A tall pine tree stood just to the right of the two chimneyed house. The windows on the second floor were, I knew, called eyebrow windows.

I had absolutely no doubt as I viewed the somewhat wistful combination of mild neglect and loving care: trim in need of paint, but window boxes filled with tulips and ivy. I could glimpse, in the back yard, part of a terrace with aluminum furniture. A negative in my mind developed into a fully realized picture: three women sitting around that aluminum table eating ham and Brie sandwiches and sipping iced tea. I suddenly and desperately wanted to be back there eating that lovely lunch, surrounded by friends with nothing more complicated to do than to decide what to pick up at the grocery store for dinner.

But an absolutely unfamiliar woman opened the door – middle-aged, plain faced and wearing a "going out" kind of purple suit.

"Is Edith home?"

After a quick glance at me, the woman made the door opening smaller. Her eyes shifted to the road to check on whether I had come alone or with an accomplice.

"There's no Edith here."

"I'm sure she lives here."

"You're mistaken."

I searched the woman's face, looking for what I occasionally glimpsed on the faces of those who were the most generous on the streets, and I found it. "Please, I know you'll think I'm out of my mind . . . ." Well I was, wasn't I? "but it's very important for me to trace the Edith who lives in this house . . . ."

"*I* live in this house."

"Who *used* to live in this house then."

"Uh look, I'm sorry. I'm on my way out. I have an appointment – "

"I won't keep you long. How long have you lived here?"

"What's this all about?"

God. It was so hard. Okay, what the hell. "I lost my memory. I'm trying to find someone who once knew me so I can – "

I gave up. My honesty was making her even more uneasy and she glanced over her shoulder as if to judge the distance to the telephone. Without knowing what I was about to say, I blurted, "Edith Waller."

She stopped trying to push the door shut and frowned. Then she repeated, "Edith Waller?" She thought a moment longer. "Look, why don't you come back later when my husband is home. He's the one who knows – "

"I don't have time."

"Why not?"

"You must have papers – records – couldn't you check?"

She glanced at her wrist. Then she tapped a bright red finger nail on a lower front tooth. "Wait here."

She shut the door and I heard a dead bolt being pulled into place. Was she calling the police? I leaned forward to knock a couple of dead tulip petals off. They dropped out of the window box onto the ground. Deadheading. I remembered deadheading flowers but could not picture the garden. Maybe I had gardened in the public parks where I had slept for who knew how long. But no, it had been my own garden. Where had my garden gone? And what an odd thing to have lost.

The door opened. "Come in."

I followed her into a small hallway facing a center staircase with two small sitting rooms on either side. She beckoned me to the right where a desk was spread with blueprints. Placing a lamp on one end and a candlestick on the other, she pointed at a corner of the top blueprint. "I *thought* that name sounded familiar. We bought the house from Landon and Edith Wallis."

A nerve began thumping in my neck. I sat down, uninvited, on the desk chair. "How can I get in touch with them?"

"I heard that Edith Wallis died in an automobile accident right after they moved and I have no idea how to get in touch with Landon Wallis. He's down south somewhere. Georgia maybe. Or one of the Carolinas."

"You don't have the address?"

"No, we weren't friends."

"Do you have any idea who their friends were?"

"No, I don't. We bought this house thirteen years ago."

I was like someone who had climbed say, Mt. Everest, nearly to the summit and then collapsed with only a hundred yards to go. The air was rare. I needed oxygen. I sat down on a chair behind me. Geometric figures danced in my head.

"Would you like a glass of water?" The woman was alarmed, torn between a desire to get rid of me and a guilty fear of me fainting.

"No, I'm okay. Thank you." I forced myself out of the chair, thanked her profusely several times, although it did nothing to allay her obvious uneasiness, and walked back to the road.

TEN

Friday, June 8
Dilly

I sticked out my tongue and felt my lips. My eyes wouldn't open. I made them. I seed wood boards and also not holes. Why they called not holes when they *are* holes? I said, "Mommy, I don't like this. Come here."

My tears all used up. I got up off the prickly burlap bag. I pulled a straw from a broom and chewed on it. An axe was hanging on the wall. Sometimes Mommy and me split wood. I use a pretend axe. I looked for something to stand on. I turned over a pail. Mrs. B. doesn't split wood any more because she's old. I tried to take the axe down. It was too heavy. I went outside and kicked pebbles. I went to the house to see if Mrs. B. comed home yet. I banged hard. No answer. Maybe she was annoyed of me. Once I throwed Curious George at her when I was pretty angry. Sometimes I'm violent. She said I forgive you. I said I'm sorry. She never gets mad. She'd come to the door if she knowed it was me. Maybe she was hiding from the Man. I yelled, "It's me, Mrs. B.", but she didn't answer.

I was hungry. Maybe I check the house. Maybe the Man goed away. Maybe even Mommy home. She'd be worried I wasn't home. Who was watering my little Christmas tree? That's what I was thinking of. It was worrying me.

I picked up Curious George and the pail and shovel. "What you like?" I said to George. "Dumplings? Sweets?" I seed a pool of water from rain it looked like. A bug was swimming. "Fish swim all day?" I asked George. "They sleep?" He didn't know.

A dog barked. I tried to whistle like Mommy but it didn't sound. A dog comed. The yellow dog. I jumped up and down. I jump a lot. "You hungry?" I asked the dog. I throwed a stick and he went after. "Bring it back," I said. He didn't know that part. I asked the dog, "You know Sir?" I said. He ran away. I heared a car going fast. Very. I hided in the woods. Only bad drivers go fast. I asked George what we do if the house not there. He didn't know. He's pretend. I couldn't remember how it was before I waked up and nobody home. Was I alone for always? Where I go when I die? Where I was before I born? Inside Mommy always? Did I wear clothes? Did I come out with clothes?

The dog comed back. I throwed a stick. He didn't bring it. "Are you paying attention?" I said. I was frustrated of the dog. I hopped on one leg. I said to George, "You wanna' carry me?" I was fooling.

When I seed the stone wall I knowed I was home. I went through the woods so the Man wouldn't see. I hided behind a tree. I watched from where not too much windows. I goed to the front. Man's car not there. Just Mommy's Jeep. I tried doors. One opened. Mommy always forgetted to lock some doors.

I was glad I was home. I putted some chicken and grapes and a carrot and banana in a bag. Cheese even. I taked the chair to the sink and drinked. I filled the tippie cup. The top screws. I taked the bag and George and Blanky and goed down the steps. I leaved the pail and shovel. Too much things to carry. I said in a grownup voice, "You hungry, George?" I said in a squeaky voice, "Thank you, Dilly. Please. You're welcome."

I put Blanky and George and the bag on the work table and climbed on the box. I pushed the stuff in the crawl space. I dragged everything to the back and hided behind the boxes. It was cozy. "Let's talk about the olden days," I said to George. "When we weren't here. We were in heaven. Somebody else live in our house. Played with our toys." I drinked from the tippie cup. Not too much. I eated some chicken. I napped. How long? I don't know. I heared somebody talking. Maybe the radio. The television. I was pretty afraid. Who turned on it? Mommy? The Man? Maybe it turned on itself. Like the TV from Sir's collar. Like the mirror Uncle Moore gave me. It makes laughing noises when you look in. Sometimes even laughs when you turn the light on in my room.

I went to the opening to hear better. The voice was louder. I hated this. I sitted next to the doll house. I looked at the teeny mommy, daddy, baby. It was too dark to see inside. I didn't want to turn on the lights. I unwrapped Christmas ornaments. I wanted to find baby Jesus. Only finded big balls. I wrapped some of them back. "Want me to read to you?" I said to George. "You make me company when I read. How your day? You go to the office? How the world started? It fell off a big ball, very hot. There was a 'splosion. When Mommy comes back I'll sleep in the middle between her and Moore. Know what stealing is? You take but don't ask.

Hook gave the crocodile his hand."

I had to poop. I listened some more. No voices. It's disgusting to poop in pants. I used to when I was little. Sometimes I wet. Only at night. I went to the opening and listened. No voice.

I climbed out. I was careful. I pooped and I almost flushed. But I remembered. I put the top down so the Man wouldn't see the poop.

Where the Man? Maybe he went away some more. It was boring down here. I want to play trucks in my room. I leaved George and the picnic and Blanky and goed up the steps. At the top I heared a voice again. It wasn't the TV or radio. It was the Man. His voice was funny. Like a little kid. Also like Mommy when she talks in her sleep. The Man asleep? I holded the banister and taked a step down. He didn't see me.

The Man said, "Father, I won't do it again. Father, stop." He cried like a little boy. He said some more, I don't know what. What should I do? I was pretty afraid. But also I was sorry. Should I tell him don't be afraid? Be brave? I didn't move. Mommy says I'm clumsy sometimes. I might make noise. I waited. Maybe an hour. Two hours. I heared funny noises. The door closed. The Man drived away I think. I was pretty happy.

SKIP

A lady said, "Is somebody in the closet?" I must have made a noise. The door banged open and I saw her. She was a coon. That's what Father calls Negroes. But only in the house. Not in front of other people. She looked nicer than Mother. She wasn't fat and she was pretty.

"What were you doing in the closet?" she asked.

"We're playing a game," Father said.

"Why are you crying? What's that mark on your neck?"

"He falls a lot," Father said. "Who sent you here?"

The lady asked, "Were you playing a game?"

"Tag," Father said.

"Can't you talk?" the lady said.

I said yes. She asked why I was crying and I said I fell. She didn't believe it. I wanted to grab her and beg her to take me away and adopt me. I could tell she was nice. Father asked her again why she was here and she said her agency got a complaint from the school. Father asked what kind of complaint. She said the teacher saw bruises. Father laughed. He said teachers were always trying to make trouble. After a while the lady left. She looked like she didn't want to leave but she didn't know what to do.

Father watched the lady drive away. He said, "I told you not to make a sound."

"I didn't mean it. It happened."

"What's that smell?" Father said.

"I couldn't help it," I said. "You wouldn't let me out and I had to go to the bathroom."

He came after me and I started running although I knew he would catch me. He said it would be worse if I ran but I couldn't stop. I told him I'd be good. I'd never do it again. Mother caught me and held me for Father.

I yelled and yelled. But nobody helped. Nobody ever helped.

ELEVEN

Friday, June 8
Faith

Years before, in a different life, I had read a book called *Eyeless in Gaza*, in which the chronological events of the protagonist's life went out of sequence, as if they had been tossed into the air and occurrences had drifted earthward in random patterns. South Springport seemed to be in a time warp, nothing in the correct order. Or else it was an outsized mental institution that encompassed a town instead of only a few buildings.

After leaving Edith's house, I walked back to town and caught a ride with an elderly woman nearly to Water Wheel. Inside Guy North's house, I leafed through the yellow pages of the local telephone directory until I found a newspaper called the Springport Express.

A man answered.

"I'd like to look through your morgue, please." (Where'd that word come from?)

"You want to consult our library?" He stressed the last word.

"Yes, please."

"Who is this?"

"Faith – " What was the name I'd given the librarian? I forgot. "Smith."

"What are you looking for?"

Good question. "I need to check some information."

"If you tell me what it is, perhaps I can help you."

"It's something I have to do myself."

"I'm sorry, Ms. Smith, we don't allow the public to consult our files."

"You used to." (And how did I know that?)

"Our policy has changed."

"Listen, Mr. uh – "

"Van Kuhn. Conrad Van Kuhn."

"Listen, Mr. Van Kuhn, this is very important."

"Why don't you give me a clue as to what you're after?"

"A crime." A crime?

"What's the name of the victim?"

"I don't know."

"The perpetrator?" He laughed. "If you'll pardon the expression."

Doggedly, I said, "I don't know."

"How're you going to look it up?"

"If I can just flip through your files, I'll know it when I come to it."

"What year do you want to *flip* through?" I could hear the irony in his voice.

"I thought I'd try the – uh – last five years."

Irony and laughter left him and his voice became businesslike. "Listen, Ms. Smith, why don't you try your local library? They keep files of newspapers."

I hung up. All I had to do was catch a cab and go back to the library.

Tires crunched on the pebbles of the driveway.

I lost all sense of direction as I dashed to the dining room at the back of the house to look out. A pond and a hill. I reversed directions. It was probably only the delivery boy. The garbage collector. Jehovah's Witnesses.

A gray Ford Taurus was parked in front and a man was getting out. He was holding the newspapers which had been lying on the driveway and he was carrying a large canvas bag on his shoulder. I careened in several directions before choosing the stairs. I was nearly at the top before it occurred to me I ought to have escaped through the back, hugged the side of the house until he was inside, and then dashed up the road. Instead, like a character in a movie farce, I suddenly dove and crawled under the four poster bed in the master bedroom.

For a time I heard nothing. What was he doing? Reading his accumulated newspapers? Unpacking? Going through the mail? Then a toilet flushed, a refrigerator door slammed, and floor boards creaked as he ascended the stairs.

Christ.

The bedsprings sagged as he sat down and dropped his shoes to the floor. Bare feet padded down the long corridor and drawers opened, hangers moved on rods. Bed springs creaked again and from under the dust ruffle, I could see sneakers. And then he was gone.

I tried to remember what I had done with the towels I'd used. Had I put them in a hamper or left them lying around? In a house as neat as this one, a loose towel was a glaring clue to violation.

Hell, what was the worst he could do? Call the police. Vagrancy was not a felony. But on the other hand, how about breaking and entering?

I smelled something cooking. Opportunity was knocking again. All I had to do was tiptoe down the stairs and sneak out the front door while he was in the kitchen. But suppose he was relaxing in the living room while waiting for his meal to cook? The window then. Crawling out from under the bed, I looked down. A long drop and no convenient trellis. Only in the movies did people jump out of windows and run away. And even in movies, middle-aged women didn't do things like that. In any case, the screen was nailed in place and there were no garden shears in the bedroom.

"Who the hell are you?" came the voice from behind me.

I wasn't nearly as terrified as I thought I'd be. Street people are accustomed to dicey situations. Besides, his voice was oddly non-threatening and non-surprised, the voice of someone accustomed to – what? Burglars? It was almost as if he'd been expecting me.

I turned around.

My first thought was, what's wrong with this picture? The man was stunted, not over five feet tall, and because he had broad shoulders and a head that belonged on a much taller man, he looked askew. It was as if a part of him had grown normally while the rest had been frozen at a critical stage by a cataclysm. He had a neatly trimmed mustache and beard and his chinos and plaid shirt were immaculate.

"I'm sorry. I can explain."

"You can?" He sat down in a chair, leaned back, and crossed his legs as if to watch a movie. "This should be interesting."

"Well, I had no place to go and I saw all those newspapers piled on your driveway – you oughtn't allow them to accumulate when you're out of town – "

"I apologize for the oversight."

" – so I knew nobody was home. I should have stayed in the barn but I was hungry – *you* apologize?"

"For allowing my newspapers to accumulate."

"I didn't do any harm. Well, maybe a *little* harm, but I can pay for the damage."

He was silent for a moment, as if he were a computer processing information. Then: "How did you pick – I mean was it only the newspapers that made you pick my house?" His voice had no tinge of regionalism or ethnic origin. It sounded like a television anchorman's.

"What else could it have been?"

"What did you mean you had no place to go?"

"I'm homeless."

"We don't have homeless people in South Springport."

"You do now."

"Where did you come from? How did you get here?"

"Boston. I came on the train."

"If you're homeless, how did you get the money for the train? Hitch? Hop a freight train perhaps?"

"I beg." I didn't think it was the moment to enlighten him about my second source of income.

"Why South Springport? Who are you?"

Why South Springport? Who are you? Easy enough questions for the rest of the world. Impossible for me. My thoughts broke off, falling into nothingness. "It's hard to explain."

"A minute ago you told me you *could* explain."

"You a lawyer? You sound like a lawyer."

He studied me a moment, his eyes moving deliberately from my disarrayed hair, to my roughened skin, to my third or fourth hand clothing, to my frayed boots. Before he could reach a conclusion, I said, "Can we, you know, sit down for a minute? What are you cooking?"

"You're hungry?"

When wasn't I? "Yes."

He turned and started down the stairs and I followed warily, like a stray dog uncertain about whether it was to be a kick or a handout. He motioned me to the kitchen table and went to the stove. With his back to me, he asked, "What's your name?"

"Faith. I don't know my last name."

"Amnesic as well as homeless?" The sarcasm in his voice reminded me of the newspaper man, Conrad Van Kuhn. Why was it that I remembered a name like that but not the name of the road I had written on the library card?

Defensively, I said, "Did you ever wake up in a strange place, not knowing who you were, what you were doing and where you had to go?"

"Me? No, never. You? Evidently you *did* know where you had to go." He brought two bowls of soup to the table and went back for bread and butter.

"The napkins and spoons are in there." He tilted his chin at a drawer in the table.

"Tell me about it," he said as I ate ravenously and he decorously.

"I woke up in a park in Boston – was it yesterday? What's today?"

"Friday."

"Friday! How much time I've wasted!"

"How much time you've wasted?"

"I had a bump on my head – here. See?" He didn't look up. "My money was gone and my mind was like – like a patchwork quilt of recycled scraps. I walked around until I came to the North Station and I saw the name South Springport and it sounded familiar so I came."

"It sounded familiar so you came."

"I felt I belonged here." I looked down at my clothes. Obviously I didn't.

"And what's your plan now? Aside from breaking into houses, that is."

"To find out who I am."

"How?"

"To keep searching until I recognize something."

"To keep searching until you recognize something."

"I take it back. You're not a lawyer. You're a voice recorder with auto playback."

"It doesn't sound like much of a plan."

He was right. It sounded terrible. It would have sounded even worse had I told him I was convinced there was something I had to do. A matter of life and death. Without asking permission, I went to the stove to refill my bowl.

"I'm hoping that if I go up and down every road in South Springport, eventually I'll recognize the house where I used to live. It's like, you know, walking up and down the aisles of a supermarket. You remind yourself of what you need." (When was the last time I had done *that*?)

The room was silent. My eyelids suddenly felt heavy and, inside my head, a faraway voice said, "*Do you hear a noise?*" For a moment the room darkened and a huge shadow appeared between me and the sky. I wished I were back on the park bench sinking into oblivion, my only problems, where to spend the night, where to get my next meal.

"– would have reported you missing. Your name and description will be on file. Faith – if that's your name – I'm not sure if this is some kind of a scam or if you're as mixed up as you would have me believe. But one thing is for sure – you can't wander the highways and byways of South Springport indefinitely. The police won't allow it."

Again I examined the odd looking man sitting opposite me who had apparently been speaking for some time. His skin was harshened by the outdoors and his small eyes were hidden by thick eyebrows, his small mouth hidden by a mustache, his chin hidden by the beard.

"You have to have *two* names in order to be in a file," I said. I didn't like the police. All the police ever did was say, keep moving, go to a shelter, get off the streets, stop hanging around storefronts, stop begging.

"Not necessarily. How many people are reported missing from a town the size of South Springport? I could try Googling you but the police could do this more efficiently."

Google me? I'd heard the word before but had no idea what it meant. He rose, and with the efficiency and rapidity of long experience, cleared, washed and dried the few dishes and utensils. Then, like a doctor stabbing a shrinking child with a needle before the latter realizes what's going to happen, he ushered me to the front door and out into the driveway. I noticed that he locked the front door. That reminded me of the broken window – another point I decided to let slide for now. He waved me into the Ford Taurus.

Suppose it was all a hallucination? Suppose I turned out to have no connection whatsoever with South Springport? Suppose there was no matter of life and death? Nevertheless, as we drove, I continued to examine houses, road signs, ponds, landmarks, fences. Now and then I received a dim signal as if I were a ham operator scanning the airwaves for a friendly voice. *Life and death. Life and death.* The words kept grinding in my brain like the clicking of train wheels.

We took Route 118 east and after a couple of miles came to the South Springport police station tucked in between a hulking Hannaford and an Advance Auto store with an ugly orange roof. We were halfway between South Springport and Freeport and had passed out of the cute zone into the modern American landscape. The police station was another nondescript brick building with fake mullioned windows that had been introduced in a half hearted and failed attempt to suggest New England architecture.

A fire fanned by the beating of my heart burned in my stomach when we got out of the car and entered the station house. A policeman sitting at a desk behind a glass window pushed back the glass and asked how he could help us. Guy North explained. Pushing a few buttons and speaking into a telephone, he summoned another uniformed man who led us down a narrow hallway which led to the back of the building. We were waved into a tiny office with a desk and several chairs.

"Lieutenant Gunther," our escort said and departed. The lieutenant, a man in his forties or fifties, had the broad shouldered, flat stomached, square jawed look of a former football player. He gestured to the two chairs in front of his desk, smiled, and sat back.

"How can I help you?" he asked. It seemed as if all the women in this town were suspicious of me while all the men wanted to help. Maybe now that I was cleaned up, I was vaguely attractive in a middle-aged, run down sort of way; it was hard for me to tell. Living an unwashed homeless life in Boston, I never seemed to arouse anything except disgust from either sex. Hadn't there been a book with a character that had an experience of this sort?

The lieutenant listened, nodded and took notes as Guy North explained, leaving out the part about my having broken into his house. Instead, Guy said he had picked me up hitch hiking on the road.

"You're sure you once lived in this town?" the lieutenant asked.

I wasn't sure of anything other than the sudden realization that the book I had been thinking of was *The Prince and the Pauper*. "Yes," I said anyway.

"Have you any idea of how many years ago that might have been?"

"No."

He leaned back, tapping his fingers on the desk. "Faith, you realize that that makes it more difficult. First, we'll see what the Missing Persons Bureau can turn up. And we'll check our own records for inquiries from friends and relatives. Various services may have filed complaints – the electric company, telephone, garbage collectors. We'll also contact the post office and the hospital – "

"How long will all this take?" asked Guy North.

The lieutenant looked at his watch. "Well, I can't tackle it right away and there's a lot of leads to run down . . . Today's Friday. I might have something for you by Monday."

"That'll be too late!"

I was as surprised as the other two by my outburst. Both looked at me with astonishment. Here they were – two well dressed, well scrubbed pillars of the community, and here I was – a miserably dressed, unscrubbed (well, recently scrubbed) vagabond telling them imperiously that that would be too late.

"Why?" asked the lieutenant.

I was silent. I didn't know.

When I didn't speak, the lieutenant said, "I'll get someone to drive you to the shelter in Portland."

"No shelter!"

Again the imperious words erupted without my volition and again they both stared. After a slight hesitation the lieutenant said, "We don't allow vagrants to wander around town."

"She can stay with me."

I looked at Guy North unbelievingly.

"She can stay with you?" the lieutenant repeated, apparently equally incredulous.

"Yes."

"You're willing to take her in for an indefinite period of time?"

"Well, you did mention Monday."

"There's no guarantee."

Guy North shrugged.

The lieutenant turned to me. "That okay with you?"

Okay with me? Stay in that airy retreat with its lovely rooms, clean bathrooms, downy beds, fragrant air, wide fields and gardens? I nodded.

Briskly, the lieutenant asked Guy North for his name, address and telephone number. He looked up. "Any connection with the North Sporting Store?"

"I'm the owner."

"How've you stayed in business with LL Bean right down the road?"

"I manage to always stay just a step behind them. When they were doing mostly hunting and fishing gear, I was doing sports clothes. Now that they do sports clothes, I'm back to hard core sporting gear. Stuff for rock climbing, white water rafting, that sort of thing."

The lieutenant smiled slightly and nodded, as if confirming something in his own mind.

Back in the car, I asked, "Why are you letting me stay with you?"

Again he shrugged.

"Suppose I'm a murderer? A thief?" Then I remembered I *was* a thief.

This time he didn't even shrug.

"But why?"

"Hey, I have empty bedrooms, lots of space. If somebody needs a place to stay, why not?"

"This town is probably full of empty bedrooms. But I doubt that too many people – "

"Also I'm obsessively orderly. If something needs fixing, I fix it. If something's dirty, I clean it. If I come across litter – "

"I'm litter?"

"– I pick it up. I have a reputation for taking in strays."

Strays. Mangy cats. Hangdog sneaks.

"Is that why you asked me why I picked your house? You thought I'd heard about your reputation?"

No answer.

"The streets of every major city are filled with people like me. How many can you accommodate?"

"Only the ones I find under my bed." This last with the hint of a smile.

Abruptly, I sat up and looked around. "Would you mind dropping me off at the library?"

"The library?"

"I want to look through their newspaper files."

"Why?"

"Wouldn't an unexplained disappearance be in the newspapers?"

"Not necessarily. Anybody can leave town."

"Without warning? Simply abandon a house, a life and leave town?"

"In any case, the library closes early on Fridays."

Roadblocks everywhere. Back at the house I paced restlessly while Guy North sat at his desk, organizing his mail. I stopped at the picture of the two Hispanic children. "Are these yours?"

He glanced up. "Not biologically or legally."

"Some more litter?"

"They live in Chile and I send them checks and they send me letters and pictures."

"Oh. You mean like 'Save the Children' or something. You ever see them?"

"I plan on visiting them one day."

"Damn!" I said.

He looked up inquiringly.

"I forgot to ask that lieutenant, what's-his-name – "

"Gunther. August Gunther."

"I forgot to ask if he would call the local newspaper, the – uh – "

"Springport Express."

"– the Springport Express and tell their editor or whatever he is to let me look through their uh – library."

"Call him. I ought to be checking in at the store. I can drop you off on the way."

The numbers of both the police and the fire departments were pasted to the base of the telephone. "Lieutenant Gunther, please."

"Who's calling?"

"Tell him I was just in to see him. Faith-no-name."

This response didn't seem to faze the operator.

"Sorry to bother you again," I said when he came on. "I was wondering – could you call the Springport Express and get them to let me examine their back copies? Maybe I'll come across something."

Slight pause. Then, "I'll do better than that. I'm on my way home and I'll pick you up and take you over."

"You will?"

"Well, you're part of my job, aren't you?"

While I waited, I went to the bathroom mirror and examined the unfamiliar image again. What was the correct image? I seemed to have had a face descent instead of a face lift. If I found my house, I would find pictures, wouldn't I? What was the name of the road I had written on the library card? I'd tell the lieutenant to ask the librarian. Or I'd tell her the truth and ask her myself. Was the library open on Saturday? The face in the mirror belonged to a woman in her forties, but the expression was that of a child, a bewildered, questing child.

Outside, I heard a car come up the driveway.

TWELVE

Friday, June 8
Dilly

I goed to the crawl space. I played with the doll house. I putted the baby in the middle with Mommy and Daddy to make him company. I hided behind the boxes. Maybe Mommy wouldn't come back. Ever. Maybe she didn't want me anymore because I be bad. What I did bad? Throwed Curious George against the wall. Once I had a tantrum and Mommy said I was a beasty. Maybe she got another kid. Chris maybe. He's badder than anybody. He pinches and says bad words. Maybe Mommy wanted a girl. She said Tracy was cute. Tracy can point out the letters in the book. I can't. She knows more numbers than me. I know about the moon walk and the astronauts. Also, which is a bulldozer, back end loader, dump truck, ambulance, fire engine, front end loader. John Deere's my favorite. Tracy hardly knows trucks. Trucks can cross the ocean if they're 'phibians. Half way they can.

If the Man comes again should I hide in the trunk? Mommy says never. You could get trapped. What was trapped? Like the water choking me? I hate that.

Mrs. B. home yet? Mrs. B said I never bad. Mommy didn't want me, I could live with her, she said. I wanna' live with Mommy. How long she away? A week? A year? I'm still a little boy. My birthday was hardly a few times ago. I had a party and a huge clown on stilts. He gived all the kids presents. A truck for me. Tracy got a pretend spider. She didn't mind. Cup cakes. I wish I had one now. Samuel gived me a earth scraper. Where it now? Maybe I have another party when I'm four. Who will make it?

The telephone ringed. I couldn't get it. I had to pee. I wished I had coffee cappuccino like in the museum. I like coffee actually. Mommy says it'll make me not grow. I had to pee so bad I let it go. I got all wet. The pee runned across the floor. The Man could see it if he comed and looked. Sometimes

Mommy says to Sir, "You drive me crazy." Man driving *me* crazy. Sir was dead. He come back? Did he like it? Mommy says if you don't like wet, go to the bathroom. Even in the night. It's hard to get up at night. Mommy still puts a diaper on me. Only at night. Mommy never gets mad when I wet. She says when I go to college I won't wet. She fooling me. She doesn't want another kid. She doesn't call Tracy Snoogums.

Come here, Mommy. I'm done hiding. I wanna' snuggle. Maybe Mommy so busy with the office she forgot she have a little kid. Mommy, I'll be good. Come here.

The wet made me a headache. Also I was pretty thirsty. My tongue sticked like the time Sir's paw goed into my mouth by accident. I wish I had a bottle. Apple juice. Milk even. At Pizza Brew they gived me orange soda. George likes bananas but I like apples. Also grapes and melon.

Tracy and Chris have daddies. I don't. He got dead in a accident before I even one. A car runned a red light. Maybe. I don't know.

Where the Man now? He hiding? I hate hide and seek. I like it with Tracy. She always cries when I yell, "Here I am!" That's fun.

Where everybody? Peg and Geoff? Susie? Moore?

I was bored of the crawl space. I goed out to the work room to listen. No footsteps. No talking. I made a drink with my hands in the sink. I played with my make believe telephone. "I wanna' talk to Mommy. How she doing? She okay? Tell me about your whole day. Wanna' play? Come on. Come on, play."

My pants feeled sticky. They smelled. Mommy makes a face when I smell. I listened. No sound. It was still day. The light comed in the basement window. Did Man go to the office? He a lawyer like Mommy? I taked the laundry cup and rinsed it. The water tasted like soap but I drinked anyway. I shut off the water. Don't waste water. It's bad for the environment.

Should I go to Mrs. B. again? It makes me tired. Maybe I ask somebody on the road where Mommy is. If I stand in the middle maybe some nice guy stop and take me to Mommy. Never stand in the middle of the road. Never go with strangers. Strangers sometimes bad. The Man a stranger?

I goed up the stairs and peeked. See if Man there. Maybe I could go out the side door from the garage. Go to the tree house maybe. Or the woods. The door to the upstairs was open. I could see bricks. No Man.

Was the Man a stealer? Stealing is when you take without asking. I taked cheese, apple and chicken from the refrigerator. That's not stealing. It's okay to take food. I putted them on the floor next to the steps and goed to my room. I slided open the drawer and taked out underpants and shorts and a shirt. I putted the wet stuff in the hamper. I got some trucks for downstairs.

The supermarket and the aircraft carrier too big. I taked a racing car. It went by remote control. Zing, bonk. It hitted the wall. It made a mark. I tried to wipe but it didn't wipe. I taked George and the truck and putted them next to the picnic. Also a book about Peter Pan. Hook cutted off his hand and gived it to the crocodile. I filled a tippie cup with water. Too much things to carry. Hold on the banister. I sitted on the top step and put the book and apple under my elbow. I made three whole trips.

How long I stay in the crawl space? I was frustrated of the Man. He was making me mad. I wished I had instructions to make a Lego train. Why Man go away when he make that funny noise?

SKIP

A funny thing happened. Father said I was faking but Mother said I was having a fit. Father said there were no fits in his family, that was ridiculous. I don't remember the fit. What I remember is feeling funny right before it happened. I was doing my homework, I heard Father come in and then I felt funny, like something was going to happen. When I woke up, Father and Mother were bending over me. First I thought they were going to hurt me and I began to cry, but they weren't. All they did was say, "Get up. What's wrong with you?" Father said I was faking and if I did it again I knew what would happen to me. I said I didn't know what I did. He yelled, "Stop faking!" and I said I wasn't faking and he hit me so hard in the face I fell. Mother said, "Never hit him on the face." Father said, "You better promise not to do that again." So I promised.

THIRTEEN

Friday, June 8
Faith

"Are all small towns full of philanthropists?" I asked Lieutenant Gunther when I got into his Ford Fairlane.

"What?"

"Guy North taking me in, you picking me up."

"Hey, I'm just doing my job."

"Taking me to a newspaper office? That's your job?"

"Keeping the homeless off the streets. Also I had another errand to run up this way."

Every now and then he turned to study me. He wasn't a man who listened superficially while his mind was on more important matters. Whether from his training at the police academy or from an innate sense of empathy, he appeared to have a habit of listening with total attention. Even to me, a disreputable fluff of dust that had blown into this clean little village from the direction of the dirty city.

"Lieutenant Gunther, is there much – "

"Since I have to call you Faith, you can call me Augie."

"– crime in South Springport?"

"We have our share."

"Real crime? I don't mean just, you know, illegal parking or drugs."

"Drugs aren't real? And why are you interested in crime?"

Why was I interested in crime? I didn't know. Not answering, I stared bleakly at the lovely white houses at the edge of the village with their white picket fences and gorgeous June gardens. The houses were so upright and proper. They belonged here as if they had grown up here along with the trees. I suddenly had a fervent, almost feverish, wish that *I* belonged here. That I had a home, and clothes and a bathtub and . . . well, everything that you were supposed to have if you were an American. It was odd, but I felt more homeless here than I could recall ever feeling in Boston. The way that (I somehow knew) women at a party felt uglier the more beautiful the women around them. We parked in front of a building which resembled a small factory or a large store.

The Junction Express was an unadorned, utilitarian space buzzing with people, computers, telephones, fax machines, copiers, but no printing apparatus as far as I could see. The press must have been elsewhere. The lieutenant identified himself and the girl at a front desk led us up an iron staircase to a second floor with cubicles. The air crackled with discussions about layouts, assignments, local meetings, photographs and advertisements. We passed several people working on computers doing what might have been layouts; two people sitting at a long wooden table discussing pollution caused by a dry cleaning establishment; a woman telling a girl to take a cab to the aquifer meeting. The only thing missing was a haze of cigarette smoke. Didn't reporters and editors smoke any more?

No one paid any attention to us except a tall slim man who hurried over and introduced himself as Conrad Van Kuhn. His was the only face that coincided with my preconceived picture of a newspaper man. It was world weary, cynical, and the mouth seemed permanently quirked at the foolishness of mortals.

"Hi Lieutenant," Conrad said, shaking Augie's hand.

Augie didn't even make a pretense of trying to introduce me. How, after all, did one introduce an unidentified person?

"Hi Connie. This lady would like to spend some time in your library."

"That makes her almost unique," the editor said.

It was odd, standing there with these two nice looking, well dressed, intelligent men. They were not the sort you routinely ran into around shelters. It felt familiar, as if I was, at last, back in my element, standing around some long forgotten cocktail party I might have gone to years ago. It would not have seemed incongruous at that moment to be holding a drink in my hand.

"We're a small paper. Of course now, everything is digitized, but all we have is microfilm from 1995 to 2000. Prior to '95, all we have are bound volumes. Come on in here and I'll show you."

The three of us walked back into a small windowless room lined with shelves of leather bound volumes. It immediately felt claustrophobic.

August Gunther looked at me and smiled wryly. "Better you than me. Do you have a way to get back to Guy North's house? If not, I can send a policeman – "

"No thank you. I have money for a taxicab."

Before leaving, the lieutenant had a brief conversation with Van Kuhn out in the hall which I couldn't hear but which I imagined went something like, "Just a harmless nut. Humor her."

I looked back and forth between the stack of ledgers, the microfilm equipment, and the computer (which I had no idea how to use) and the word Sisyphus floated into my head but who was Sisyphus? Not an old neighbor. Someone in a book.

"Are you good with a computer?" Van Kuhn asked as he came back into the room. "You might as well start with the most recent issues."

I shook my head.

"Ok, let me show you how to use the microfilm then."

He patiently sat down beside me and showed me the drawers of microfilm, removed a tape and threaded the film through the proper passage. Then he indicated the start button, the forward and backward mechanism, and speed control.

I thanked him profusely. He waved a hand as if to dismiss the thanks and left. Once I was alone, I regarded the machine much as I might have a lion which I'd been assured was tame. Finally, I ventured a tentative stroke. The pages whipped past frantically. I slowed it down. A judge brought up on ethics charge; recycling drive coordinated among the villages in the township of South Springport; two high school students chosen for a statewide concert; a party for a popular school bus driver about to retire; a conflict management training session for district administrators, teachers and school board members; a meeting of the historical society to discuss better record keeping; local boy finishes second in Florida golf tournament; ambulance volunteers putting on a demonstration for school children; advertisements for restaurants, hairdressers, lingerie, water softeners, the "next generation" of antiques and Guy's sporting store. Births, marriages and a dating service: "Skip the cute part and cut to the chase. I'm beautiful, slim, thirty-four, a tennis player, a skier. How can you resist? I love music, plays, ballet, art exhibits."

Peoples' lives sped past me on the pages. They were long lived around here; many seemed to make it to 90. It reminded me of a cartoon I had seen long ago of someone reading an obituary page where each obituary headline read something like "4 years older than you", "10 years older than you", or more frightening, "10 years younger than you." Where had I seen that cartoon? *Yes, the New Yorker*, a voice in my head answered.

The more recent obituaries included pictures of the deceased in their younger years, always laughing or smiling. These struck me as even sadder than the pictures of old people, their eyes barely visible behind thick glasses, the deep lines from their noses to their mouths charting the trajectory of their descent into death.

The pages swirled by on the screen. My eyes began to blur and my attention wavered. An elderly couple murdered by a religious gang from Boston. A woman sodomized and strangled by her gardener. Four year old boy, Adam Meservey, found tortured and murdered by "the fly" killer. The murderer's signature, a dead fly, pinned to the child's chest.

Suddenly I was descending a hill in a world filled with puffy gray mists. I grabbed hold of prickly raspberry bushes and immature maple saplings to keep from sliding down too quickly. An amber colored deer raised its head to watch me and then, flinging up its rear hooves, disappeared in a flurry of white tail. Underfoot, the ground was spongy with moss as I approached a stream. I had to hurry, stop dawdling. I was wasting precious time. I followed the stream as it wound among the trees until I found a narrow ford and jumped. On the other side the land ascended precipitously to a pine cathedral carpeted with needles. As I walked, a small mound bundled against my chest made a soft bleating sound.

Memory is a chain. Grab one link at a time and you can reach the end. Try hard enough and you remember your passage from the womb.

"Is something wrong?" I was startled to hear Van Kuhn's voice behind me. It was not unkind, just harried. I realized that I was slumped in my chair, no longer looking at the microfilm machine but instead, staring at a wall. He regarded me doubtfully, a reluctant foster parent faced with an unattractive charge.

"No, no, I'm fine. Just tired, that's all."

"Like some coffee?"

"No, thank you." I had to escape the buzz of the machines, the non-stop voices, the confining space, the warmth of the room. "I wonder – can I take a break and come back later?"

"Sure thing."

Outdoors, I took deep breaths of air. It was like the shelter. I had to get out.

What now?

Try to find the wooded area with the stream and the steep hill and the pine forest? How? It wasn't too different from the land behind Guy North's house. No. That hill was much steeper. Perhaps if I went up and over his hill . . . .

I went back into the Springport Express office and asked the girl at the reception desk if I could use her telephone. She waved at one of the desks. "Press nine and then your number." I asked for information, got the local taxi service, and told the dispatcher where I was to be picked up.

The driver arrived in under ten minutes. "Twelve dollars," he said when I gave him Guy North's address.

"Twelve dollars!"

He didn't bother arguing. Simply turned away with a bored expression and waited.

I got in the cab. He ignored me. While he drove, I searched in my stolen wallet for the exact amount, not trusting him to give me change of a twenty. I found a five, six singles and four quarters.

We were about a mile out of the village when my attention was caught by a church. It wasn't the white steepled one in town but a smaller granite one I had glimpsed on my arrival in town. Not knowing why, I said sharply, "Let me out here."

"It's still twelve dollars, Lady."

Without debating the point, I handed him the bills and silver and walked up a flat driveway to the church. Opening the doors, I saw a pleasant, white painted interior with maybe fifteen rows of pews, two aisles, a balcony for the organ and choir, and a modest altar. Like other aspects of the town, it was both familiar and strange.

I left the church and continued up the driveway to the stone parish house. Inside, the carpeted hallway led to a large dark hued painting on the opposite wall of the Virgin and Child. Did I remember this particular rendition or only the general subject?

An electric typewriter clicked down the hall and I followed the sound to an open office. An elderly gray haired woman in a striped blue and white cotton shirt and a blue cotton skirt stopped typing and looked up. "Yes?"

"Uh, Mrs. – "

"Lamonagne."

"I used to live in South Springport and I've been trying to trace . . . have you lived here long?"

"Twenty-two years. Why?"

To hell with it. "Do I look familiar to you?"

She stared. Slowly, she said, "Should you?"

"I lived here once."

"How long ago?"

"Uh, long ago."

She glanced at the papers beside the typewriter and then, reluctantly, she got up. "What's your name?"

Shit. "I used to be a member of this church and I was wondering if you recognized me."

"Are we playing games?"

I took a deep breath. How had I gotten off on this tangent?

Stick to the newspaper office. Search the land behind Guy North's house. "Well, if you don't remember me . . . ."

She came closer. "As a matter of fact – "

"Yes?" My chest was beginning to hurt.

"I'm not sure. At my age, well I see a familiar face and I can't recall if it's someone I know from the checkout at Hannaford's, or – or a cocktail party acquaintance – " Suddenly, her expression changed so drastically, it was as if she had turned into someone else.

"What?"

"I – no. I'm mixing you up. I thought for a minute – you reminded me – "

"I reminded you of whom?" I hardly recognized my voice.

She was beginning to look bewildered. "What did you say your name was?"

"Who do I remind you of?"

"I made a mistake."

I was exhausted. All I wanted to do was escape. Why did I keep this up if I didn't really want to know the answer?

"I'm sorry I interrupted your work. If you should remember, would you call Guy North's house?"

"Guy North? Of North Sporting Store?"

"Yes. I'm visiting him. I'm a, uh, relative."

"Yes, of course. I made a mistake."

Outdoors, I sat on the steps for a moment to rest. Why had her face altered so violently when she had thought she recognized me? She had looked almost horrified. But then she had turned doubtful. Genuinely confused.

Join the club.

I began walking. My fatigue was only emotional, not physical. I turned left on Route 120 and headed towards Guy North's house on Water Wheel Road. But then, impelled by the amorphous memory or vision I'd had in the newspaper office, I continued past Water Wheel Road. I passed Pepper Ridge and was approaching the Route 118 turn off when I saw it. The name of the road I'd written on the library card. Salmon Kill.

FOURTEEN

Friday, June 8
Dilly

I never sleeped so much in my life. I waked up and looked at the crack to the outside. What time it was? What day? I forgot. Every day get fresh air, Mommy said. I goed to the crack to get fresh air. Plants and trees make fresh air.

I don't like hiding. I want Mommy. Also lobster. Not chicken all the time. I'm bored of this. Nobody entertaining me. No treasures in the crawl space.

I listened. No sound. Did the Man drive away? Maybe the Man went home. He have a home? I comed out of the crawl space and jumped on the floor. Maybe I call zero and somebody find my Mommy. Actually, I'm really bored of this. I'm only a little boy. I goed up some of the stairs and the Man said, "Well, well, well, you here all the time."

I was scared. I didn't know what to do. I couldn't run even.

The Man was standing on top of the stairs. He was smiling. I hated his smile. I said, "I want my bottle. Also George."

He said, "Anything else?" I didn't know. He comed down the steps. I thought of something else. "My Mommy."

"Why you hiding?" he said.

I didn't know.

"Where you hiding?" he said.

I didn't want to tell.

He said, "You'll tell father sooner or later."

I said, "You my father?"

"I look like your father?" he said.

"I don't know."

"You don't know your own father?"

"He dead," I said, "in a automobile accident."

Man said wise father knows own son. What that mean? He said, "Come upstairs."

"My things in the crawl space," I said. "I wanna' stay there."

He said, "So you hiding in the crawl space."

I said, "How you know?"

"Get your things and come upstairs."

I said, "Help me," but he didn't. I carried myself, Curious George, Blanky and some of the picnic.

He said, "A balanced diet. You take a course in 'trition?"

I said, "What's 'trition?"

He didn't answer. I eated an apple. I said, "You a bad guy?"

He said, "Nobody's perfect."

"I want milk," I told him. He didn't get it. I dragged the stool to the sink and drinked water. I carried some to the table. I didn't spill.

"You have a house?" I said.

"Your mother lending me this one."

I cried. Only a little bit. It made me choke on the apple. "You know my Mommy?" I said.

He didn't answer.

"Where she is?" I said.

"Soon you be with her."

"She coming home? Now? Soon?"

"No. You go to her."

"I go now?"

"Not yet."

"Why?"

"First we have fun."

"Why Mommy go away?"

"She sick."

"How she sick? She have belly ache?"

"She visit the undertaker," he said.

"What's undertaker?"

"Somebody takes care of troubles."

"Like a doctor?"

"Better. She had terminal headache."

I said, "What's terminal headache?" He didn't answer.

I said, "She coming home regular time tonight?"

"What's regular time?"

"Seven most times."

"Where she work?" he said.

"At the office." Then I remembered. "Not this week. She on vacation." I gived the Man water. "Have a sip. It'll cool you off." He didn't.

I said, "Take the seeds from my apple." He didn't. "You wanna' play?" I said. He said yes. I jumped up and down. Mommy calls me Jumping Jack sometimes. "Wanna' play tractors? Come. Come." We goed to my room. I told him, "This is hydraulic lift. The stabilizers come down. You can play with the front end loader. Wanna' share? I take the dump truck." I putted the plastic village on the floor and zoomed the dump truck round the school and the post office and the fire station.

"Why you not playing?" I said. He didn't answer. "This truck crosses the ocean. It's 'phibian. I have a idea. You call the restaurant and get us spicy Japanese food. Beer for you, orange soda for me. Cindy does that. I'm bored of chicken."

"Who's Cindy?" he said.

"My babysitter. She not here because Mommy on vacation."

I heared a car. Man went to the window. I told him, "It's the mowers. I don't like that racket." The Man pulled down the shade. I said, "Zoom, zoom, shoot, shoot. Don't kill him. He has parachute. Pretend you the daddy. I'm the mommy. We have three children. George, the rabbit and Sylvester."

"Who Sylvester?" he said.

"He's a bear. Know what you should do? Read to them."

He didn't.

"You wanna' invite Tracy?" I said. "We can have a play date. Hey! Don't do that. I don't like that."

The Man stopped.

"In the olden days we were dinosaurs," I said. "Then came babies. In these days cars and trucks. You like sweets? They make your teeth yellow. Not if you brush. You have some sweets?"

He didn't answer. I drawed on my construction paper. "You can make me company while I draw," I said. "See this? It's Japanese writing. I'm writing a letter to my Mommy. Dear Mommy. Why you not come? I can't read the letter. You read it to me."

He didn't.

"Cindy always plays with me," I told him.

"You like Cindy?"

"I *love* her."

"She come often?" he said.

"She come every day. Not weekends. Not when Mommy on vacation."

"Your mother have a cleaning woman?"

"I had a hair cut," I said. "I was pretty brave. I don't like those guys. They do a bad job." I putted the pencil in my mouth. "I'm smoking. Only pretend. You know this guy, Curious George? I'll introduce you. Know why I don't want a sister or brother? Those guys grab a lot."

"Which day the cleaning woman comes?" he said.

"I forget."

"Today's Friday. She come Friday? Saturday?"

"What age you like? Soon I be four."

"Your sitter coming back Monday?" he said.

"I'm bored of talking. Let's play."

"You have grandmother?" he said. "Grandfather? Relatives?"

"Peg and Geoff. They live in 'chusetts. Wanna' play pirate ship?"

The Man said, "Let's play hide and seek."

I said, "I don't like that idea. It's a bad idea. When we were at the store, I nagged Cindy for sweets. She said Mommy have a fit. I told her hide sweets in back on top shelf. You go see if any left, okay?"

The Man went away. I said, "Man, where you go?" He didn't answer. I picked up crayons and drawed. I listened. No sound. I goed to the closet and put on my baseball cap. It's my favorite. I heared a sound. I said, "Man! Answer me! Where you are? You make me mad. Come out!"

He didn't. I taked a crayon and throwed it at the wall. It made a mark. I was sorry. I went to the sink and drinked more water. I taked George and Blanky to my crib. I throwed Blanky inside. Then George. Next I climbed. "Wanna' play, George?" I said. He said yes. "I call the restaurant. They deliver. That a good idea?"

Man made a sound. I climbed down and runned in Mommy's room. "Where you are? I hate this."

"Come find me," he said.

"You annoying me," I said. "I don't like this idea. Come here!" He didn't. I cried. I went to the 'frigerator for chicken.

"Here I am!" The Man yelled so loud I dropped the chicken. He comed back. Don't eat food on the floor. I don't care. I picked up the chicken and eated some.

"Want me to tell you a story?" the Man said.

I said yes.

"Sit on my lap."

I didn't like that idea. He made me.

"This a story about a fly."

"Mommy vacuums flies in vacuum cleaner," I said.

"One day the fly was captured – "

"Like Hook captured Peter Pan?" I said.

He said "Keep quiet." He was rude. "The fly was captured by a huge black and yellow wasp."

"Why?" I said.

"The wasp stabbed and paralyzed the fly."

"I know what paralyzed is. It's not moving."

He said, "The wasp taked the fly to his underground house. Like a dungeon. He sticked wasp eggs to the fly. Fly waits three days in dark."

"Why he not have flashlight?"

The Man said, "When the wasp babies born, know what happens?"

I said, "You know the tooth fairy? She comes at night. She gives you a quarter if you lose a tooth. I'm too little yet."

The Man said, "When the wasp babies born, they eat the fly while he alive."

"He alive?" I said.

The Man said, "The wasp babies eat the fly while he alive and fresh. A little at a time."

"That the whole story?" I said.

He said yes.

I said, "Does the fly like it?"

The Man laughed. He had white teeth. He didn't eat sweets. I heared a sound. What kinda' sound? I don't know. He said he had to go away.

I said, "Who baby sit me?"

He said I a big boy, take care of myself.

"I'm too little," I said.

"Take a nap and wait for me."

"I don't like that idea. What if it's a fire?"

"You'll be cooked," he said.

"What you mean?"

"Wait for me. Don't hide."

"I wanna' go with you."

He looked outside. No more mowers. "You hide, I paralyze you," he said.

I cried. "Bye, bye, Man."

"Don't worry. I be back," he said.

SKIP

Father said, "The bitch left. She packed everything she could lay her hands on. The only thing she left was you."

At first I didn't understand. But I didn't ask questions because questions always made him mad. Everything made him mad. It was better to say nothing. Sometimes saying nothing made him mad.

"Aren't you interested in the fact your mother took off?" Father asked me.

"Took off?" I said.

"What the hell is wrong with you? I always told the bitch you were a moron but she kept saying you were really smart. What's dumb if you're smart? Your mother left us. Get it? She vamoosed, skipped, skedaddled."

"Mother went away?" I said.

"You have it at last," he said. He spelled it. "W-e-n-t a-w-a-y. You always got good marks in spelling."

"When is she coming back?"

I should have stayed quiet. He grabbed my arm and twisted. "God, you're stupid," he said. "I don't give a damn she's gone. What bothers me is she forgot to take you. I'm stuck with a brain damaged kid."

Did I love my mother? She never kissed me or hugged me. But she was my Mother. The only one I had. Who would take care of me? Who would shop and buy me clothes and take me to the dentist? Not that she had done much of that.

But now I was all alone with Father.

I looked at a picture on the wall. It was supposed to be Father's ancestor. But it was a fake. He bought it in Vermont. I wasn't brain damaged but I was too dumb to stay quiet.

"Who will take care of me?" I asked.

He began yelling. "Who'll take care of you?" He said it maybe five times. "In some countries, kids your age work on farms or in factories seven days a week, ten hours a day."

"What'll I do when you're at work?"

"What makes you think I'm keeping you? I'm thinking of taking you to an orphanage."

An orphanage! An orphanage was probably like the hospital where people were nice and gave you presents. I could read and watch TV. He must have noticed how happy I looked because he said, "On second thought, I can't do that. It would give people the wrong impression. I'll keep you around to do the cooking and the cleaning."

"I'm only a kid. I don't know how to cook and clean."

"You'll learn."

"Who'll take care of me?"

"Who takes care of the little coons in the city? They take care of themselves. Only you won't be doing what they do. Selling drugs and sticking knives into people. You'll go to school and when you get off the bus you'll do your homework and then the housework."

Then he said, "And if you don't do exactly what I say you know what will happen." He had that look on his face. Like he hoped I'd do something bad.

"And you know what else?"

I didn't say anything and he yelled, "I asked you, do you know what else?"

"No."

"You won't tell anybody about any of our private business. Don't even say your mother's gone on a trip."

"Okay."

"It's just you and me now."

I couldn't help it. I began to cry. I tried to choke it back but I couldn't. Father watched me and smiled. He reminded me of a monster coming out of the ocean, reaching out to drag me down to the bottom.

FIFTEEN

Friday, June 8
Faith

The name on the mailbox at 140 Salmon Kill was Cushman. Cushman? It was a pretty pink brick two storied structure. Attached to the left hand side was a white one and one-half story structure with eyebrow windows. Along with "eyebrow windows", the words "summer kitchen" jumped into my head. Two marble slab steps led to a front door of polished oak.

I walked down the short drive past a neat lawn between two old maple trees, past some lilac bushes and hydrangea bushes, up the steps and knocked.

No answer.

As if on automatic, I continued to the back where the lawn sloped down into woods. The snarled images in my head – real or imagined – were so intertwined I couldn't unravel them. I walked into the woods. It was a new forest with brambles and maple saplings. I saw a chair resting in the crotch of a tree where hunters waited for deer to appear, and then came to a stream where a half rotted log provided access to the other side. Here was the land ascending to the pine forest where I had walked with a small, warm bundle hugged to my chest.

I walked back towards the house. As I emerged from the woods, two women appeared on the road from around a bend, one young with a pony tail hanging down her back and the other middle-aged with short hair, both dressed almost identically in brightly colored tee shirts, shorts and jogging shoes.

"Hi there," they said cheerily and almost simultaneously, but they couldn't resist glancing at my rusty jacket, long skirt and boots. The sight of them shook me free of whatever spell gripped me and I walked the rest of the way back to the pink brick house. As I approached the front of the house, I saw a Volvo station wagon parked in the driveway. For a moment I hesitated in the shelter of the trees at the side of the house. It was acceptable to approach a house from the direction of the road, quite another matter to emerge from the resident's private woods. I could hear voices from an open window, a child's and a woman's. They sounded like disturbing yet unfamiliar ghosts from a former existence.

I scuttled towards the house. Because the land descended away from the side of the house, the side windows were relatively high. By keeping close to the house, I could creep around to the front without being seen from the windows. Then, pretending I was coming from the road, I knocked on the door again.

A pleasant looking woman in her thirties wearing a plaid skirt with a navy blue sweater, a black hair band on her head, opened the door. Attached to her side was a little girl also wearing a plaid skirt and a hair band. They looked almost ludicrous and yet I immediately envied them their nearly matching mother-daughter outfits, their brightly colored tights, the financial security that made it possible to think about things like matching hair bands.

"Mrs. Cushman?"

"Yes?" She examined me doubtfully, but the child smiled with open friendliness.

"I once lived in this house and I happened to be passing and couldn't help stopping to see it again." I hadn't planned this speech. It just came out like a rushing stream.

"You lived in this house?"

"Yes, that's right."

"When was that?"

Where was the rushing stream now?

"Some time ago. May I come in and look around?"

"Well, I'm pretty busy. I'm expecting my husband any minute and I'm fixing – "

"I won't stay more than a minute or two. You know how it is. Once you've lived in a house, you can't help feeling curious about the changes the current owner might have made." I had an inspiration. "You know Guy North who owns the North Sporting Store?"

"Not personally, but I know who he is."

"If you call his store and ask for him, he'll vouch for me. Faith." Sure. Why not? He was a perfect reference. All I did was break into his house, smash a window, take a bath.

Mrs. Cushman teetered on her moral fence for a moment and then fell over on my side. "Come in."

I walked into the front hall. On the left of a front hall was a living room with a chintz sofa and armchair, a small oriental rug in front of a brick fireplace, a clutter of children's toys, books and puzzles. Off to the right of the front hall was a formal dining room with a large mahogany dining table and beyond that, I could glimpse a kitchen. A graceful, curving flight of steps led from the front hall to the second floor. My first thought was how lovely it was, how lovely it would be to live in a place like this with real plaster moldings and a real slate roof and a dining room table for, well, dining.

My next thought was that while the furniture, the paint, the curtains were all unfamiliar, beyond the superficial differences, there was something about the layout and the atmosphere which singed my nerve endings. I walked into the living room. Mrs. Cushman followed me, clearly wanting to keep an eye on me without being obvious about it. Feeling nauseated, I sat down on the sofa without being asked.

"How long have you lived here?" I asked abruptly. It was time *I* did some of the questioning.

It was the child, not the woman who answered. "Before I was born. I'm five." She smiled with the friendliness of a little girl who had never had reason to doubt the goodness of the world.

"Seven years," Mrs. Cushman said.

"From whom did you buy it?"

"Look, I have to fix dinner. My husband will – "

"Mrs. Cushman, I haven't been honest with you."

She bent down and lifted her little girl into her arms.

"I'm perfectly harmless." Well, maybe not to screens and windows. "I've lost my memory but I have a feeling I once lived in this house. If you tell me the name of the former owner I may be able to find out who I am."

"Family by the name of Bossica."

No whiff of memory.

"What were they like? I mean, could one of them possibly have been me?"

"Oh no. They were an older couple. Much older than you."

"Do you know how I can get in touch with them?"

"They're both dead."

"They're dead *too?*"

"Too?"

"How did it happen?"

"I told you they were elderly. At least in their eighties. The wife died just before we bought the house. Cancer. And the husband died not long after in

Florida. From what, I don't know."

"How did you hear he died? Were you in touch with him?"

"I heard it from an older woman who was a friend of theirs. She goes to the same church as I do."

"What's that woman's name?"

She hesitated. Then, "Louise Skoglung."

"Do you have her telephone number? Address?"

Had I always been this aggressive, this persistent? Or had these personality traits developed on the streets? Mrs. Cushman glanced helplessly back and forth between me and the child as if seeking advice. Torn between the desire to be rid of me and the reluctance to involve an acquaintance with a lunatic, she chose the former. She disappeared in the direction of the front hall where I had seen a phone on a front hall table and a few seconds later, the little girl wandered back out to the living room.

"I go to kindergarten," the child said.

"Do you like it?" I noticed that the mother was keeping an eye on us as she leafed through a phone directory.

"Uh huh. I like story hour best. How old are you?"

"I don't know. How old do you think I am?"

"You don't know?"

"Here's the Skoglund number," Mrs. Cushman said, handing me a piece of paper.

The little girl tilted her head to one side. "You're older than Mommy but younger than Grandma."

"Tina!" Her mother exclaimed.

"Mrs. Cushman, may I make a call from here?"

She exhaled a whoosh of air from her lungs. I could see she was about to refuse but I couldn't spare the time. I slid past her, picked up the telephone and dialed. An elderly voice answered.

"Mrs. Skoglund?"

"Yes."

"I'm trying to trace a family who once owned the brick house on Salmon Kill. One forty Salmon Kill," I added, recalling the number on the mailbox. "I think their name was Bossica."

"Why?"

I went through my tortured explanation. When I was finished, Mrs. Skoglund said crisply, "The one who might know who owned the house before the Bossicas is their son Stephen. He's a partner in a law firm in Boston. You can find him in the book."

I thanked her fervently and before Mrs. Cushman could work up the nerve to stop me, I flicked through the Boston directory, found Bossica & Bossica, and dialed. The female who answered wanted to know what my business was with Mr. Bossica.

"It's personal and it'll only take a minute."

With unexpected promptness, a male voice said, "Steve Bossica."

"I'm sorry to bother you, Mr. Bossica," I said hurriedly, my eyes pleading as they met Mrs. Cushman's. "It's very important for me to find out from whom your father bought his house in South Springport."

"What's that? Who's this?"

I was close to hysteria. In a singsong voice I repeated my story.

Silence. Then, "Miss – "

"I told you. I don't know my name."

"Okay, Miss Jane Doe, in the first place I don't answer questions on the telephone – "

"All I'm asking is from whom did your father buy his house?"

"– and in the second place I have no idea if you're really who you say you are or if your story is a whole bunch of malarkey. You want to talk to me, come to my office on Monday. I'll see if my secretary can squeeze you in."

"But I'm in South Springport and I don't have the time – "

"What's the hurry?"

"Mr. Bossica, how can it hurt you to save me the time and trouble of going to Boston by just telling me the name of the family from whom your father bought the house?"

"And in the third place, Miss Jane Doe, I don't know."

It was like a kick in the stomach. I felt dizzy and lost my breath. Through a haze I could still hear him speaking. "– wasn't as if I was a kid when they bought the house. I wasn't living with them and it never occurred to me to ask them from whom – " I could hear the mockery in his voice as he imitated my peculiarly formal grammar "– they bought their house."

Furiously, I said, "Then why did you just tell me to go to the city – "

"To be accurate, I said if you wanted to talk to me, you could come to the city."

I waited for control. The walls seemed to be tilting like those in an amusement park fun house. Tina and Mrs. Cushman had signed up as cast members for the nightmare and were all askew, stretched out of shape. "Mr. Bossica, you suggested I waste an entire day and go to a great deal of trouble to see you and yet you had no intention of helping me. What kind of a person are you, Mr. Bossica?"

The child was staring at me, open mouthed, and the woman was beginning to look as harried as I felt.

Bossica sounded amused. "Listen, Jane Doe. I'll show you what kind of person I am. And without billing you. Take yourself over to the town hall, tell them the location of the house, and they'll give you all the information you need. Property ownership is a matter of public record."

The room and its occupants straightened out and I could breathe again. Why hadn't Lieutenant Gunther suggested that? Why hadn't Guy North?

Because until this moment I hadn't known which house had once been mine. Which house I *thought* had once been mine.

Faintly, I said, "Thank you, Mr. Bossica. Thank you very much."

"My pleasure, Miss Doe. And if you're ever inclined to waste an entire day and go to a great deal of trouble, I'll take you out to lunch and you can tell me what this is all about. And again, no charge."

I hung up, and without giving Mrs. Cushman a chance to protest, leafed swiftly through the local telephone directory. South Springport, town of. Building inspector, court clerk, fire department, highway department, planning board, police, receiver of taxes, recreational department, supervisor, town clerk.

Town clerk.

"Town clerk," a voice said after one ring.

"I'd like to trace the ownership of a house on Salmon Kill Road. One forty Salmon Kill."

"Call the tax assessor's office."

"Could you transfer me, please?"

"You're too late. The office is closed for the weekend. Try Monday."

Too late. Too late. Too late. The words revolved in my head like the clicking train wheels. I wanted to start screaming. Stamp my feet. Yank the telephone off the wall and hurl it through a window. Throttle the amused Mr. Bossica. Shake the innocent Mrs. Cushman.

But not her child.

"Monday will be too late."

"Too late for what?"

"Would it be possible for me to get the home number of whoever is in charge of the tax assessor office?"

"No, I'm afraid not. And as a matter of fact, I have to close up now too." Click.

I continued standing at the telephone, staring sightlessly at a sketch hanging on the opposite wall. And then not sightlessly. With sharpened attention, I went over and examined it closely. An innocuous landscape.

"Mrs. Cushman, where did you get that sketch?"

"What? Listen, I really have to start – "

"I'm about to leave. Honest. No more telephone calls. Just tell me where you got that sketch."

"It was here."

"Here?"

"I found it along with other things in the attic. I rather liked it and had it framed. Why?"

"Thank you, Mrs. Cushman. Thank you for putting up with me. And you too, Tina. Thank you for saying I look younger than your grandmother." Impulsively, I leaned down and kissed the little girl before her mother could stop me.

SIXTEEN

Friday, June 8
Dilly

I writed a letter to Mommy. "Dear Mommy, how you feeling? How your day? Tell me about your whole day. Let's talk and stuff. You see Tracy? I very brave. If you think I like this you totally wrong. I want a gun when I grow up. When I'm five. It's a long time from now. I don't want a sister. I shoot targets. Not people. I got to go. Come see me."

I looked at the letter. I couldn't read it. Was it right? I made a picture for decoration. I have artists in the family. My uncle. He lives in Denver.

I zoomed my John Deere. I jumped up and down. "Fire! Be careful. Boom. Prepare for takeoff. Throw a line. Get the people out. George, you 'cited? George, pay attention."

I got bored of that. I was never alone before. In olden days always somebody. Mommy said, "Good morning, Dill Pill. Ready to face the world?" Mommy teases. She has humor. She swings me up and down with her feet. Sometimes we build castles. She says, "Pack wet sand. It holds better." She makes battlements and moats. Sometimes a monster in the moat.

Was the Man coming back? I don't like him actually. He's okay for company. He bothers me. I like Cindy to baby sit me. Where she is? Mommy on vacation. Cindy never baby sits when Mommy on vacation.

I looked out the glass next the front door. The door was locked. You pull the button and it opens. Same with French doors. Should I go out? I could if I wanted. The Man said wait. Mrs. B. home yet? I taked off the telephone and said, "You wanna' talk?" Nobody answered. I pushed buttons. The buzz stopped. Nobody there. I putted it back. Never leave the telephone off the hook. Where's the hook?

A jay pecking the ground. I said, "Hi, bird. I have a idea." I goed to the greenhouse and opened the bag with seeds. I taked two hands full. Seeds falled out, but not too much. The jay flied away. I said, "Come eat," but he didn't. I guess he wasn't hungry.

I put on the light in my room. The mirror laughed. Uncle Moore gived me the laughing mirror. It scares people. It laughs when you look inside. Sometimes laughs when the light goes on. It scared Tracy once. She cried.

I went outside. I pulled the button so I could come back if I wanted. I told George to stay inside. It was getting not light outside. I goed down the driveway. Only a little way. Was Mommy in Denver? She never went before without me. Once, maybe. But Cindy babysitted. Where Cindy live? I could visit. I don't know. Sometimes I say I don't know when people ask even if I do. But I really *don't* know where Cindy lives. I kicked pebbles and throwed a stick. No Sir to fetch. Sir dead. Maybe he get undeaded. I checked. Be careful. Never go near water. Never, never, never, never. Don't push emergency buttons. Don't touch matches. Ever. It's dangerous. It makes a huge 'splosion.

I picked a dandelion and tasted. It didn't taste much. I sang Old McDonald. I don't know much songs. I watched a dragonfly. It was pretty interesting. They sting. They like wasps? Eat flies? Don't step on plants in the rock garden. Only rocks. I checked the pool. Only from far away. Sir still dead. It was getting dark. Was it night time? Maybe Mommy come home regular time today. Maybe I go to Mrs. B. before dark. I told the dragonfly I used to have a Mommy. Once we had a horse in the barn. Not now. We selled it. Lots of jumps in the paddock. Policemen can go past stop signs. They have permission. The front door of the barn was hard to push. Instead I goed to the back behind the barn. Some old tires and rusty machines. Mommy said Good will take it way. Why? Who Good? The grass was tall as me. I brushed away from my nose. I taked a berry off a bush and tasted. "Never eat anything unless I tell you," Mommy said. "Even banana?" I said. That was a joke. I spitted the berry. Thorns scratched. Something stinged me. I yelled. A bee flied away. My hand hurted. I cried and rubbed it. I hate bees. They do bad things. Also wasps. Mommy wasp paralyze the flies. Then her baby wasps eated the flies alive.

I turned the faucet outside the barn. I putted cool water on the sting. It was all red. I drinked from the spigot. Mommy said never touch spigots with lips. Germs on it. I peed on the grass. Maybe I go back and eat something. Get George and Blanky and sleep outside. Too much mosquitoes. I can't hide in the crawl space. Man knowed it. Maybe I could watch some TV. Maybe get in my crib? Man be angry because I leaved the house? I rubbed where the bee stinged me. It was getting big.

I was pretty sleepy. The barn is okay. The Man couldn't find me. I pushed hard on the door. I squeezed in. It was dusty on the floor. A spider builded a huge web on the ceiling. It was interesting. I could see something in the web. A fly. Spiders eat flies too? Should I save the fly? I looked for something to stand on. Nothing. I couldn't reach.

I taked the horse blanket from the wheel barrow and finded a place to nap. Most of the barn was filled up by a old sailboat belonged to Uncle Moore or my Dad or somebody. I don't know. It was all cracked and dirty. The mast leaned. Maybe I could camp until Mommy comed back from vacation. Like a cave. Man wouldn't find me. I could play hide and seek from him.

Was the Man bad? I don't know. Maybe he could tell me more stories. Maybe he could cook a egg. A steak maybe. I was pretty tired. In the morning I could visit Mrs. B. Maybe even Mommy come home.

Cement floors are hard. But they're sturdy. How you make cement? I seed a rabbit through the door. It hopped. Once Sir catched a rabbit. I looked at its insides. It was pretty interesting.

I dragged the horse blanket to the boat. Maybe I sleep inside the boat. Maybe under so Man wouldn't find me. I bended to look under the boat. I yelled. A hand was under the boat.

SKIP

Am I like other kids? I don't think so. I have thoughts nobody else in the world has. I don't tell anybody about them. I act polite and friendly but I don't get close to the other kids.

I'm the only one I know keeps a diary. I'm not sure why.

Whenever I'm going to faint I have a warning. I can't explain the feeling but it gives me time to get away from people and be alone. Nobody ever catches me.

I think maybe Father damaged my brain. Is it possible? I'd like to get my hands on something smaller than me and do things I don't want to talk about. Like what Father does to me. Only worse. Is that insane? I hate Father. Why do I want to do what he does? I can't understand it. Maybe I'm crazy.

SEVENTEEN

Friday, June 8
Faith

Between the dark and the daylight,
When the night is beginning to lower,
Comes a pause in the day's occupations,
That is known as the Children's Hour.

Where did *that* come from?

South Springport's twilight was an intermingling of beckoning pathways and forbidding labyrinths. Returning to Guy North's house, I passed a trail illuminated by the last rays of the sun. It disappeared into a pale green woodland. I hesitated a moment, transfixed. There was something both beautiful and terrifying, attractive and repulsive, about that trail into the woods. I might have been sirened off the road if I hadn't been pressed for time. I hurried past.

Back at Guy North's house – he had given me a key – I went straight to the telephone. The desk sergeant wouldn't tell me Lieutenant Gunther's home number, but said the lieutenant would call me as soon as possible.

While I waited, I went to the bathroom for a pain reliever and popped two Tylenols into my mouth. I washed them down with water and combed my hair. It was important to blend in with the normal residents of South Springport. But what constituted a normal resident? Was the woman with Alzheimer's a normal resident? Did *she* blend in?

The telephone rang.

"It's Augie Gunther, Faith."

"I found the house I used to live in!"

"You sure?"

"I'm . . . well, I'm almost sure. No, I'm sure. If I can get into the tax assessor's office, I can find the names of all the former owners and then I'll know who I am."

"You'll recognize the name if you see it?"

"Don't you think so?"

"Well, don't get too excited. There'll be a lot of red tape. Finding people who knew you, proving – "

"The first bit of red tape is that the tax assessor's office is closed until Monday. The reason I called is that I want to ask you to get them to open it for me tonight."

"Hey, I don't know if I can do that. I mean, under such uh – ambiguous circumstances – "

"It's important."

"Can't it wait until Monday?"

"No, it can't."

A slight pause. Then, gently: "Faith, I'd like to help but no one is going to believe this an emergency."

"But it *is*!"

"How? What will happen if you don't find out who you are until Monday?"

"The police can do it. I'm sure it's easy in a town like this for you to go to whoever's in charge and ask for a favor.

"Okay. I'll do my best. Which house do you think is yours?"

"The brick one on Salmon Kill, 140 Salmon Kill."

A pause. This one longer than the first. Then: "I'll call you back."

I paced like a prisoner in a small cell. I examined the child's antique fire engine next to the staircase, the small sculpture of a rural scene with the two grazing sheep, the lithograph of the Penobscot River.

I lay down on the sofa and tried to relax. Fat chance. The telephone rang and I sprang up.

"Faith, this is Guy – "

"I'm sorry, I can't talk to you. I'm expecting a call from Lieutenant Gunther."

"That's why I'm calling. He wanted me to explain to you that there's nothing he can do. You'll have to wait until Monday."

I was silent. Control was important. I mustn't do or say anything to create the image of a mad woman. "Why didn't he call himself?"

"He was nervous about your reaction. He thought that since I knew you better – " he laughed, a bit grimly I thought "– I might be able to convince you that there's nothing to be done until Monday."

When I remained silent, he continued. "I'm coming to get you."

"Get me?"

"I'm picking you up."

"Why? What are you going to do?"

"Wait and see."

I lay back down on the sofa, exhausted. What did he have in mind? It was easy to imagine that he'd reached the end of his rope with me. I'd broken into his house, perhaps overstayed my welcome and meanwhile, I was harassing his neighbors and town officials while acting strangely all the while. I was like a puppy that one adopts on impulse and then instantly regrets taking in.

Was he going to deliver me to a shelter? If I made a run for it, where would I run? This town was where I had to find my answer and I was too tired to search for another house in a condition suitable for breaking and entering. Images tried to wedge an opening into my mind, but as soon as they gained a foothold, they were sucked out again as if by a powerful vacuum. I could hear screaming. A high pitched shrill voice maddened by agony. A huge dark shape blotting out the night sky. A distorted head, masked by a stocking. Wires tightening around my wrists and ankles as I struggled convulsively like a small animal in a trap trying to tear off an appendage in order to free itself. The long mournful wail of a train whistle. A dirty carpeted floor, passenger seats, a rocking motion, darkness interspersed with coruscating flashes of light.

"You fell asleep."

Guy North was standing over me. I struggled to a sitting position. He was dressed in preppy outerwear and looked as if he were about to attend a rowing regatta: a blue fleece, neatly pressed khaki pants, boating shoes. It was incongruous with his odd body shape.

"Let's go," he said.

I rubbed my face as if to remove an unpleasant coating.

"Where?"

"You'll see."

"I won't go to a shelter. Or some miserable hospital with dirty walls and people yelling."

"Which hospital is that? It certainly doesn't sound like our local one."

My head was filled with an out of control cartoon that featured scenes from my dream as I followed him out to the car. I was still massaging my face, trying to shed an unendurable outer skin.

"You're certain you once lived in this house on Salmon Kill?" he said as soon as we were on our way. His voice sounded odd, just as the lieutenant's had when I'd mentioned the address. What did they both know about that house?

"I – yes. I also recognized the land behind it – the woods and a stream."

"A lot of the land around here has the same contours."

"Also the layout inside was familiar. Only the furniture and paint were different."

"Lots of traditional houses have similar layouts."

"Why is everyone trying to talk me out of it? What did Lieutenant Gunther say?"

"He said it would take a court order to open the tax assessor's office tonight. He doesn't have grounds for that."

"Suppose it were a matter of life and death?"

"Whose life? Whose death? You're only trying to find out who you are."

I shut my eyes to combat the dizziness. A huge, indigestible lump was growing in my stomach.

"I wish I could wake up from this nightmare."

"If this is your nightmare, what happens to me when you wake up?"

I glanced over at him but he was smiling as if he had just asked an amusing riddle, the answer to which I did not know.

Houses streamed by, lamps behind translucent curtains revealing shadowy figures. The headlights lit up huge branches that arched over the road like a vaulted cathedral ceiling. In this kind of town, they didn't cut down the old trees to make way for the electrical wires. People were willing to put up with occasional electrical outages in order to preserve the old maples that lined the roads. Out on Route 118 we passed the Hannaford, Advance Auto, and the police station. On the outskirts of Freeport, we stopped in front of the North Sporting Store.

"What are we doing?" I asked.

"We're choosing an outfit for you."

"I don't have enough money – "

"You think I'm going to charge you? Next you'll be expecting a bill for room and board."

"You're giving it to me free?"

"Jesus. Let's go."

"I don't understand you. I break into your house, you think I'm crazy, and yet you're giving me clothes."

"It's no big deal. I get it wholesale. And you'll do a lot better in your – uh, investigation, if you look like you belong."

The North Sporting Goods store was housed in an old fashioned barn.

It looked like what I imagined LL Bean looked like a couple of generations or so ago. Although how did I suddenly know what LL Bean looked like? It was a big building with uneven wooden floors. I looked around and saw camping gear, sleeping bags, a corner with compasses, topographical and trail maps, another with rows of hunting guns.

A tall, handsome young man, maybe in his twenties, approached us. He wore a tight white tee shirt, cargo pants and hiking boots. Perfect health and fitness seemed to radiate from him like an electrical field. I suddenly felt shrunken and withered.

"Can't keep away, can you, Guy?" he said.

"We're going to take a look around in the women's department."

The three of us walked to the back of the store where I was surprised to see a small but varied assortment of women's sportswear.

"Why don't you look around? We're getting out of this business but we have a few things left," Guy said to me as he moved out of earshot to talk to the young salesman.

I remained where I was. The few customers still in the store at that late hour kept glancing covertly at me. The young man disappeared and returned with an equally perfect specimen of young feminine beauty.

"Come with me," she said. She led me to a small dressing room with mirror, bench and hooks. "Take off your clothes. I'll be right back."

Feeling like a prisoner about to undergo a strip search, I sat down and tried not to look at the wall mirror. I didn't remove my clothes.

"Here we are." Her arms were loaded with sportswear: pants, tops, sweaters, and even some sports bras and skimpy underpants that seemed designed for mountain climbing or some other activity I would never engage in. She avoided looking at me, behaving in the manner of a mistress, in a reversal of fortune, compelled to wait upon her housemaid.

"I could only guess at your size so I brought an assortment."

She was gone again and I continued sitting. Moments passed. From the other side of the door, she asked, "How're we doing?"

"I don't know."

The door opened and she stared in astonishment. Also irritation. "Aren't you going to try anything on?" She handed me navy blue slacks and a white cotton over blouse. "These look like they might fit."

I waited for her to leave. Then I removed my familiar long skirt, yellowed blouse and loose jacket and surveyed my disreputable underwear. I removed those also and when I found some that fit, I put on the new underwear, slacks and over blouse and also a navy blazer. Good enough. Folding my old belongings into a tight bundle, I left my sanctuary. She was waiting. "Guy said you're to take several outfits."

"This is all I want."

Shrugging, she handed me a hairbrush. "I'll take those things." I yielded my belongings as if surrendering a baby and she accepted them as if they were toxic waste. When she returned without them, she said, "Shoes are next. What size?"

"I don't know."

The shoe clerk brought out four pairs of navy flats and some knee socks and when I found a pair of shoes that fit, the young saleswoman whisked away my boots.

"Now, how about a sweater or two at least?"

"No, I don't need one. Thank you."

Guy North examined the new me. With a noncommittal "Let's go," he led me back to the front of the store.

We came back through the store a different way than we had gone in, through the middle of the tent department. There were several tents set up on the floor and a couple hanging from the ceiling. I glanced away from them to a counter that held a glass case with knives in it. One of them caught my eye. A Buck Fixed Alpha Hunter. Not very subtle. I wondered how many of those they sold to women. When I glanced back at the tents, a small blond boy, maybe about five years old, was emerging from one of them, blinking as if he were awaking from a dream. My vision blurred and my head suddenly lolled forward. I staggered and Guy caught my arm.

"What's the matter?"

I waited for the floor and my stomach to stop heaving.

"Can we go?"

"Sure, come on."

Guy guided me out of the store, his hand on my elbow, and to his car.

While we drove back in silence I considered the pros and cons of breaking into the town hall. It would be harder than a private residence. It wouldn't have easy-to-snip screens or easy-to-break glass. It would probably have an alarm system. And once inside, how would I know where to look?

"We're here," Guy North said.

"Here" was a parking lot behind the Hannaford shopping center. He held the back door and I walked into a large, dimly lit, carpeted Oriental restaurant. We were escorted to a small table with a pink tablecloth and fresh flowers. Informally dressed couples with small children occupied most of the other tables, but dotted among them were men and women in business suits.

The maitre d' – if I knew that, then surely I hadn't always dined in shelters and bagel emporiums – handed us menus and left. While Guy North studied the menu, I studied a toddler sipping a pink concoction topped by a cherry and a tiny paper umbrella.

"Would you like a drink?"

Tearing my eyes away from the toddler, I said, "I seem to remember a train. A train going through the night. Lights shining in my eyes. It was speeding and I rolled back and forth."

Why didn't I tell him about the other memory – the screaming, the intolerable crescendo of agony and fear? The distorted head and the looming monstrous shadow? Perhaps because if I didn't put it into words, it would go away. It would recede into oblivion along with the rest of my past.

The waiter returned with two glasses of wine and I fingered the stem of the glass without drinking any. "I was lying on the floor of the train. My head hurt so much I thought I would – "

"You were lying on the floor? You mean you were on a freight train?"

"No. Passenger. Like an Amtrak train. I kept hitting the seats when the train rocked."

"How did you get on this train?" He stopped to order some food from a waiter who seemed inordinately interested in our conversation. "Did you have a ticket?"

"I was carried on."

"You were carried on." His voice was flat, non-committal. "Who carried you on?"

"I don't know. My head throbbed and my wrists felt like they were burning – " I examined my wrists. I saw nothing but blue veins.

"Wouldn't somebody have noticed?"

"It was late. Maybe there wasn't anyone around to notice."

"How about the conductor?"

"I could have been thrown on when he wasn't looking. When he was in another car."

"God knows that could happen on Amtrak. I never see a conductor on that train once they grab the ticket from you. So you think you were thrown on?"

"That's my impression – " The waiter brought soup and I began to eat. It was better, much better, than the soup in the shelter.

"You sure you didn't dream all this?"

I was silent. Everything I said was dismissed as delusive. And why not? Someone like me was hardly a reliable witness. We finished our soup and the waiter brought us two platters with unidentifiable – at least to me – morsels of fish in one and greenery in the other. Guy North spooned samples of each on our plates.

"Don't you want wine?"

"I have to have a clear head."

Guy gave out a snort of laughter.

After a couple of minutes of silence, he began to speak again. "You know the old saying about learning to swim in the winter and skate in the summer?"

I continued eating ravenously.

"Meaning, that in the winter, when one doesn't swim – "

"What about an indoor pool?"

"– one absorbs the lessons one has learned in the summer. Whereas in the summer, one absorbs the skating lessons of the past winter."

I said nothing.

"For instance, in my case," he went on, "I always play a better game of tennis after I haven't played for awhile."

"You ought to spread the word among the big name players. Save them a lot of time and effort."

"What I'm saying, Faith, is give it a rest. Don't try so hard to remember and maybe it will come to you all by itself."

"Why is everyone so anxious for me not to know who I am?"

He put down his fork, wiped his mouth with his napkin, and turned his palms heavenward. "That's not true. All we're doing is trying to help you."

Give it a rest. Don't try so hard. It will come to you all by itself.

Well, in a way it had, hadn't it? South Springport. Salmon Kill Road.

I sat back and suddenly I was filled with the simple pleasure of having eaten a good meal in a pleasant room with a companion. It was luxurious, literally beyond any dream I could recall. To live this way, to wake up healthy in a pretty house in a quaint town, spend the day working in an office or a store, and then to drive in absolute comfort to a restaurant and eat a Chinese dinner. Surely, this must be the apotheosis of all civilization. Desire for anything beyond this was greed and the cause of all poverty, war and human misery in the world.

The trouble was, I had to hurry. My lofty philosophical thoughts dissolved. Whatever I was seeking was a matter of life and death. I would have to do it by myself, just as I had done up to now. Without their help. Without Guy North. Without Lieutenant Gunther. Without the newspaper man, Conrad Van Kuhn. Without Mrs. Cushman or Mr. Bossica. Without the tax assessor, whoever that was.

God helps those who help themselves.

Guy's credit card and the paid bill had been placed at Guy's elbow.

"Come on," I said, getting to my feet, "we should get going."

EIGHTEEN

Friday, June 8
Dilly

A real hand sticked out under the boat. Not Halloween. I yelled, "Mommy! Wake up. Come here. Please." She didn't. She was stuck under the boat. I couldn't move her. I runned around the boat. I jumped up and down. A squirrel was bothered. I had a tantrum. I kicked the grass. Mrs. B. wake Mommy up? It was a long way. It was getting night. I could get lost like Hansel and Gretel. A witch could come. A bad guy maybe. What bad guys do? They shooted guns. Make people dead. What dead? Mommy dead? The Man kill her? My throat hurted from yelling. I seed an ant crawl on Mommy. I tried to catch it. It got dead by mistake. It didn't move. I goed to the pool to see if Sir better. Still floating. Another thing floating. Maybe a mole. I tried to catch it with the pole. Too heavy. Was the mole dead too? Everybody dead. I goed to Mommy and taked her hand. It was cold, I shaked her. She was really stuck. I wished I had something to eat. I was bored of chicken. I prefer dumplings. Like at Red Dragon.

A car comed. I runned to the woods to hide. I heared garbage cans. The garbage man was nice. On Christmas Mommy gived him a check and he gived me a duck. It walked when you winded it. I said thank you. He said you're welcome. I runned out of the woods to the driveway. The truck was disappeared down the driveway. I yelled. The man didn't hear. I goed back to Mommy. Some of her hair peeped out under the boat. It bleeded. I went to the pool. I found the chlorine cup. I kneeled down beside the pool and washed the chlorine cup. I was careful. I didn't lean much. I swished the cup and filled it. I carried with both hands and poured on Mommy's chin. Only that part of her face showed. Nothing happened. I remembered the spigot. I filled the cup again, poured more on Mommy. She didn't wake up.

I heared crickets. Probably one was Jiminy Cricket. A airplane went by. In the olden days Mommy and I went on airplanes. Not propeller. Jet. I eated

THE FLY MAN MURDERS

steak and laid on the seat with George. Where I leaved George? Mommy readed me *The Lorax*. That's Dr. Seuss. Bad guys killed all the trees. I wished she could read right now. I was too tired to look for George. Maybe I go in the house and eat something. Maybe the Man there. I curled up close to Mommy. It wasn't cozy. She didn't tickle. I taked her hand and snuggled.

I waked. It was almost dark. I thought I was in Mommy's bed. I was wet. She didn't like that. Most of the time she didn't let me sleep in her bed. Big boys sleep in their own beds. I hate growing up. I don't want to be a big boy. Sometimes at night I throwed Blanky and bottle and George over the side. I comed down and carried my stuff to Mommy's room. I tiptoe so she won't hear. I lied down on the rug next to her bed and sip from the bottle. George cuddles me. I sneak back to my crib in the morning. Sometimes Mommy wakes first. She says, "Snoogums, you little creep, who said you sleep here?" What's a creep?

I was thirsty. I looked around for a bottle. A tippie cup. No bottle. No tippie cup. I putted some water from the spigot in the cup and drank that. It tasted bad. I spitted it out. Mommy still asleep.

The huge spider was still in the web on the ceiling. I could still see from the light in the sky. A rope comed out of the spider. The spider climbed down his rope to the boat. The boat was dirty. The spider didn't care. I asked Mommy to wake up. She didn't. Maybe she would come back never. Never. I cried. "Where you go, Mommy? You in heaven? Can I come?"

I was hungry. I wished I had something to eat. A cricket chirped. I couldn't find it. Maybe it talked like Jiminy Cricket. It was a conscience. A conscience tells you if you're bad. A robin cheeped. Why a robin awake when almost night? I drinked from the spigot. I spilled more water on Mommy from my hand. No use. I pooped in the woods. It's okay. Not like litter. Never touch spigot with your lips. Get germs. I don't care. I seed a cat in the bushes. He scare the robin?

Automatic lights goed on in the house. The Man inside? Playing hide and seek? Who take care of me when Mommy dead? I seed kids from Africa or Indiana or someplace on TV. No food, no house, no Mommy. Who take care of them? They take care themselves? How? I have no Daddy. Now no Mommy. Maybe Cindy take care me. Maybe Geoff and Peg. That's my grandmother, grandfather. I want Mommy.

I cried. I never cried so much in my whole life before. I seed a deer. He was coming close. Deers don't hurt. Only they eat Mommy's bushes. I wished I had Mommy's BB gun. She shooted a squirrel. The squirrel tried to take the bird food. It didn't kill. Only stinged. "Go away," I said to the deer. "Don't eat

Mommy's bushes." The deer standed on its back feet and runned away.

Deer have babies?

"I'm too little take care of myself," I yelled at the deer. He didn't care.

I wished I had lobster sauce to eat. What's lobster sauce? You put it in the trap and the lobster eat it? Maybe I do Mommy a favor. Put clothes in the washer. She be proud of me.

I heared a sound. Who made it? It was like Sir. In his sleep. A squeak. Maybe Sir done with being dead. I was afraid. Not brave. Mommy calls me a wimp sometimes. I know what wimp is. Somebody not brave.

Mommy's fingers moved.

I yelled. I jumped up and down. "You're not dead, Mommy!" I never so happy in my whole life. I stopped yelling. I seed if the Man back. I didn't want him know Mommy not dead. Why? Maybe he make her dead again.

"Mommy, how you feel? You feel fine? Don't be dead, Mommy." I pushed her chin. I goed for more water. I sprinkled on Mommy.

I heared the squeak again. I rubbed her chin and kissed it. I wished I knew 'susitation. 'Susitation is how you make people alive when dead. I wished I knowed how to call the doctor.

I ask the Man to call the doctor? He wouldn't. He was bad. Like a wasp. I wished I was four. Then I know what to do.

I lied next to Mommy. I tried to make her warm but she was under the boat. I was hungry. I was afraid to go to the house. I wanted to stay close to Mommy. I patted her hand. I made her company.

SKIP

At first I hated the amusement park. It was crowded and hot and noisy and no fun. The only reason Father took me was this guy from his office took his kid and asked Father to take me. Father patted me on the head a lot. Which I really hate. He called me Son. It was so phony I don't know why the other guy didn't catch on. Father is a phony about a lot of things. He tells people he only watches news on TV. But he likes horror movies. The other kid ate a hot dog and coke and ice cream. Father said they were bad for me and besides I ate at home.

I think a lot about Father dying. He could get cancer from smoking but that took a long time. Maybe he'd fall asleep when he was in bed smoking and he'd burn up. He talks a lot about me burning in hell. Once he was under the car fixing something. I thought about getting in and running over him. I know how to start a car. I could tell the police Father forgot to put it in park and it slid over him. Who'd suspect his own son? But I was afraid he might not die. I got sick thinking of what he'd do to me. If it was so bad when he had no reason, what would happen if he had a reason? A big one?

The other kid said, "Let's go on the roller coaster," and his father said, "Why don't we all go?" I didn't want to. When Father saw I was scared, he said, "Sure." I wondered if the bar would hold me. What if I couldn't hang on? What if I flew over the top? But I couldn't say no. Father would get me when we were home. It would be worse than falling out of the roller coaster. I was really nervous. I guess all my life I'm nervous.

The roller coaster started up slowly. I was so afraid I was shaking. Father watched me and he had that look on his face. I held on so tight my hands hurt. I asked God to take care of me. That was a joke.

"It's beautiful up here," Father said. "What a view." We were sitting together. The other kid and his father were behind us. We started going faster. I slid down in the seat and my teeth hurt from holding them so tight. We went higher and higher. I was sure I'd fall out the minute we started down. I could hear the guys up front yelling when they went over the top. I could hardly breathe. I closed my eyes and waited to smash on the ground.

We went over the top and something funny happened. The air whooshed on my cheeks and I felt like I was flying. Not like on a plane. I was never on a plane so I don't know what it's like. But this was like flying with my own wings. I even opened my eyes and I started to tell Father I liked it. The wind took the words away. Then I saw Father's eyes were closed and his face looked like mashed potatoes.

Father was afraid! He was afraid and I wasn't. Once he said I was a puppet and he pulled the strings. I thought, he's the puppet now and I'm pulling the strings. It was the happiest time of my life. I watched him sideways. I was ready to turn away if he opened his eyes. We climbed another hill and Father's lips moved like he was praying. Did God listen to him?

I thought about giving him a push when we got to the next high point. But I didn't know if I was strong enough. Besides, the guys behind us would see.

When we got off Father pretended he liked it. I could see he was really mad. He was going to blame me. He was going to say I was the one wanted to go on. He'd make me pay for it.

Some day I would make him pay for it.

NINETEEN

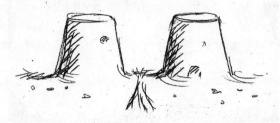

Saturday, June 9
Faith

I was peering through a lattice work of fingers and a childish voice was prattling, "This is the church. This is the steeple. Open the doors and see all the people." The child's face was amorphous, like a fetus in amniotic fluid waiting to be born. A small prenatal hand reached out to me imploringly.

The scene changed. I was wearing a wool hat, nylon parka, corduroy slacks, leather gloves, thick socks, ice skates. Clutching my hand was a Lilliputian stumbling along on double runner skates and threatening to fall with each frantic lurching step. There was no delight on the small face, only dogged determination. The two of us kept to the fringes of the pond, out of the way of the more accomplished skaters.

Next I was whisked to a candlelit restaurant, other diners' faces floating about like balloons. A backhand symphony of soft voices and the tinkle of cutlery and crystal rippled smoothly around us. An aura of happiness and safety filled the room as the waiter poured champagne.

"To the little he or she about to join us," someone said, holding up a glass. "Have you chosen a name yet?"

The name curled out of the champagne glass like a genie and the candle sputtered and waved and the air vibrated.

"Robert!"

"What are you yelling about?" a voice asked. It was a voice out of another dimension.

I sat up in bed. An oddly shaped man, almost a dwarf, was standing in the doorway, silhouetted by the light behind him.

"Robert?" I asked and the genie and the candle and the champagne and the soft glow and the murmur of warm soft sounds evaporated.

"What did you call me?" the silhouette asked.

Who was this intruder who had ripped me out of that bubble of happiness into this strange small white room? I wanted no part of him. What I wanted was to slip back to that other world where none of it, whatever it was, had happened and the future could be remolded and corrected by the right choice instead of the fatal one.

"You were shouting in your sleep and when you saw me, you called me Robert."

It was all gone, the aura faded, paradise lost. "I'm sorry I woke you."

"Who's Robert?"

I lay back and looked out of the window. It was dark outside. The sky was a black gauze sprinkled with Christmas lights.

"I don't know."

"What were you dreaming?"

Faint outlines shimmered, sensations more than visions. "I can't remember."

After a moment he said, "Would you like some hot tea or cocoa?"

"Thank you, no. You're awfully good to me." I made my voice sleepy sounding and manufactured a yawn. "I'm so tired."

The silhouette didn't move. Then he said, "It's four in the morning. I may not be here when you get up. Saturday is a busy time at the store."

"Please don't bother about me. I'll be fine."

He was reluctant to leave. "You can have eggs and there's a French bread for breakfast. Since you can't go to the tax assessor's office today, what will you be doing?"

"I'll read." Oh sure.

Another pause. "If you need me, I left the number of the store by the phone. You might want to – uh, go to a hairdresser or something. I have a charge account with the taxi company and the hairdresser can bill me."

"It'll take more than a hairdresser to do me any good." I tried to laugh.

He stood there another few seconds, as if he were uncertain about leaving. I felt a tension rising in me, as if the room were suddenly filling with water and I might, at any moment, need to crash through a window to escape. Just as my nerves were being stretched to maximum tensile strength, he finally left. The light in the hall went off, the stairs creaked as he went upstairs, the bedsprings squeaked. I waited for about ten or fifteen minutes and then, silently, slid out of bed. I was wearing a pair of Guy North's pajamas and I folded them neatly and put on my new outfit. Then I made the bed.

Was this the last time I'd sleep in this room? The last time I'd be in this house? The last time I'd see Guy North?

Why should that be?

I didn't know. Logic didn't come into it. My head was spinning out of control, about to loosen itself from my spine and disappear into space. Everyone seemed intent upon thwarting me, holding me down, pumping mists into my head. And yet, at the same time, needles punctured my skin as if I were undergoing acupuncture. Hurry. *Miles to go before I sleep.* (Why were these echoes coming at me faster and faster? Because I was finally near my home?)

No sound from above. Gently I unlocked the front door. Then I remembered the master bedroom faced the driveway. Suppose Guy North were looking out?

What if he were? Why the sneakiness?

Nevertheless I went out through the side mud room towards the barn, keeping to the back. Once past the barn, I went out on the road. I walked down Water Wheel towards Route 120 and turned right. Only my feet seemed to know where I was going. They arrived at the intersection of Pepper Ridge, the road just before Salmon Kill. I knew, without knowing, that the two ran parallel. On impulse I decided to see what was behind "my" house.

It was on the edge of dawn. There were few houses on the road. On my left a gravel driveway circled away into the darkness. I knew I had to go further in order to be in back of my house. At the top of a hill, I came to a flat stretch with a modest red house on my left fronted by a white picket fence, behind which was a cottage garden that nearly filled the small front yard. Even in the pale light, I could see it was blooming with irises, delphiniums, late tulips, June roses, poppies, and flowers I couldn't identify. Vestigial memories told me that every bit of it had been painstakingly sculpted to create these waves of color and shape.

Something about the garden was incongruous, however. It took me a moment before I realized what it was. In the midst of the immaculate display was a carelessly dug up area featuring two sand castles connected by a scooped out indentation.

If the castles had been real, with arrows bristling from battlements and alligators lurking in the moat, I couldn't have been more transfixed. A drill of pain bore through my body.

BUITENKAMP was the name etched in black lettering on a red letterbox meant to resemble the house. Buitenkamp? Features struggled to appear as if in a photographer's chemical bath but the chemicals were defective. I couldn't match the name with a face.

Despite the fact that dawn was just beginning to pale the sky, I went to the front door and knocked. While I waited, I pulled on the neck of my over blouse as if it itched, which it didn't, and wiped my eyes as if they were tearing, which they weren't. I rang the bell, banged. Windows opaque with drawn curtains. No other evidence of a child in sight.

Looking through a window into the empty garage, I spotted what I considered another incongruity. The garage was as excessively neat as the garden, but a burlap bag had been dumped carelessly in the center, and there was an indentation on it. As if a dog or a cat had been using it as a bed. Or a child.

Again I was overwhelmed by a sense of impending disaster. Emanations from the violated garden, the shuttered windows, the indented burlap bag all made me tingle with a sense of urgency. Hurry, they were telling me, hurry.

Although I had left Guy North's house only a short time before with the sense that some cataclysmic event might prevent my return, I now hurried back. On Route 120 I encountered another insomniac with a yellow Labrador Retriever on a leash. As he drew closer I recognized the newspaper editor, Conrad Van Kuhn.

"Small world," I said idiotically.

"Small town," he answered. In the faint rose gray light his tall thin frame appeared to be slightly phantasmal. I could see how handsome he must have been perhaps fifteen or twenty years ago. He was still handsome in an austere way.

"You never came back to the newspaper office," he said. "Did you find what you were looking for?"

"Not yet, but you said I could return if I had to."

"Any time."

"You live around here?"

He pointed in the direction from where I had come. "Near the village."

"Do you always walk your dog this early?"

He looked almost abashed. "He's young. Not yet a year. My wife had her heart set on a yellow Lab but I'm not sure we did our homework properly. We seem to have acquired one of the stupidest dogs that ever roamed the Earth."

"You know, I think I've seen that dog out on its own running around."

"Undoubtedly. He runs right through the invisible fence. If we tie him up with a rope, he chews through it. We're going to have to build a fence, a big fence. The other problem is, he wakes up at five a.m. and barks incessantly until we take him out. So I have to walk him at this ungodly hour. At least

"No."

I realized that the conversation had taken a turn, that it was no longer a coincidental meeting between neighbors at an odd time in the morning. I was being interrogated. No, I was being interviewed. For a story in the paper.

"Listen, come on back to the paper on Monday," he said. By now I felt most as if he were leaning towards me. "Maybe we can help you search the chives."

I instinctively backed up a step.

"Oh thanks. Maybe I will," I said.

He frowned, realizing he'd gone too far, too fast. I turned, waved, and rted walking away. I felt his eyes on my back as I walked.

Back at Guy North's house, I called out but he didn't answer. I checked barn and saw the car was gone. Saturday was a busy day, he had said. I some breakfast and waited until I thought the police station would be n.

I dialed and asked for Lieutenant Gunther. I didn't care that he was going e sick to death of me.

"Who's calling?"

Faith."

Faith who?"

thought of answering "Faithless" or maybe "Faithful" but since I didn't which I was, I just said, "Knock, knock" and giggled foolishly.

he police in this town were definitely accustomed to weirdos. "The nant is off today."

lease. Tell him to call me."

hen I hung up I went through my usual routine examining the re, lingering at the picture of the "adopted" children, inspecting the fire engine. I studied the book shelves for the first time: sets of s and Trollope. *The Impossible Voyage* by Chay Blyth, *The Ambassador* ry James, *The Clown* by Henrich Boll, *Appointment in Samarra* by John , *Broca's Brain* by Carl Sagan, *Bellefleur* by Joyce Carol Oates, *Nineteen* *Four* by George Orwell, *Buddenbrooks* by Thomas Mann, *Siddharthat* nann Hesse, Peterson's *Field Guide to the Stars and Planets*, *Fables and* *les* by Leo Tolstoy, *The Manticore* by Robertson Davies, *Gulliver's* y Jonathan Swift.

rited or selected? Why would I assume a small town sporting store ouldn't be a reader?

telephone rang. I ran to it.

tenant Gunther?"

at this time of the morning, I don't run into a lot of neighbors w
training advice, all of it conflicting."

I laughed. He was such a pleasant man away from his hectic w
had the bizarre thought that maybe I had once been married to a
this. Although I was sure that we'd never met until this week.

"So, where do you live?" he asked.

I blinked. No one had asked me where I lived for many ye
always been self evident that I lived nowhere.

"I'm just visiting. I'm staying with Guy North."

His eyebrows went up. "Oh? Are you a friend of Guy's?"

"Well, yes." It would have been awkward to explain tha
intruder.

"Do you know Guy?" I asked on an impulse as the mem
strange figure looming in the bedroom doorway came back to

"Oh sure. Guy's not exactly a 'man around town' but I sho

"What do you mean, 'not a man around town'?"

"Oh you know. He doesn't hang out around bars, that sor
did you say you met him?"

"Oh, I also shop at his store and . . . so I know him . . .

A second rise of the eyebrows. I could appreciate that
to understand how one went from shopping at his store
house.

I changed my mind about trying to get him to tell me
But, as it turned out, Van Kuhn was more inquisitive than

"So what were you looking for in our archives? Mayb

For some reason, maybe because of the odd circums
dawn meeting, I was reluctant to tell him.

"Actually, it's a pretty complicated story."

"Really? You've piqued my curiosity." He paused and
to take another tack, he said abruptly, "Lieutenant Gun
victim of some form of amnesia."

It was slightly alarming to think how many people
of my odd situation by now – notwithstanding that I
been telling the story to almost everyone I met. "Wel
live here."

"But you don't know your name?"

"It might have been Faith."

The dog was pulling at the leash but he ignorec

"But you don't know your last name?"

"How did you guess?"

"I'm really sorry to keep bothering you but there's something I want to show you."

"What?"

What indeed? A child's sand castle. A burlap bag.

"You still there?" he asked without impatience.

"Lieutenant Gunther – "

"Augie."

"I was walking along one of the roads around here and I came across something odd."

"Yeah?"

"I'd rather show you than tell you. It won't seem like anything if I describe it. You have to see it for yourself. Can you come here?"

"Sure."

"Thank you. Thank you very much."

I continued pacing. It was a commonplace assumption that one could tell character from the books one owned. What was Guy North's character? My mind raced, but in several directions at once. Who were the Buitenkamps? Who was Robert? How could I get hold of the tax assessor?

Guy North called and I told him about the sand castles and the burlap bag and calling the lieutenant.

"And he's coming over?" he asked.

"You sound surprised."

"I thought the police were too busy giving out parking and speeding tickets to bother with sand castles."

The sarcasm surprised me. I was silent.

"I called to see how you were getting along," he said.

Impulsively I said, "How kind you all are! You, the lieutenant, even that newspaper editor, Van Kuhn. How helpful." Except that I wasn't getting any help. "I have to go now. The lieutenant is here."

He was driving a red Subaru. I recalled that he was off duty. As I got into the car, I said, "I was just telling Guy North how kind you all are."

"Neither rain nor snow nor gloom of night, oh right, that's the postal service. Where to?"

"Pepper Ridge. Were you able to do anything about getting them to open the tax assessor's office?"

"I can't convince anyone it's an emergency."

"It's the house at the top of the hill. On the left. Buitenkamp."

He parked on the short driveway and I led him to the front garden.

"The owner is obviously away. Now, notice anything out of the way?"

Baffled, he looked at the garden, the mailbox, the shuttered windows. Some of my certainty leaked away.

"Isn't it strange to find a child's sand castle in a perfect garden?"

"This is what you wanted to show me?"

"Come with me." I led him around to the garage and pointed to the burlap bag with the imprint on it. In the full light of day the outline didn't seem quite as self evident.

"Doesn't that look as if a child slept on it?"

"So?"

"Well, a child doesn't belong here. At least there's no other sign of a child. You know, swings or bikes, or whatever. And what mother would allow her child to dig in someone's neat garden?"

"A not very nice mother?"

The starch was draining out of my body.

Gently, he said, "Faith, what does all of this have to do with *you*? With discovering your identity?"

I was like someone speeding at full throttle and slamming into a concrete wall. Confusion and pain hit me with an almost physical force. "I don't know. Probably nothing. I was just being a concerned citizen. Isn't it a matter of – uh – public interest to investigate the possibility of a small boy wandering around alone?"

"Boy?"

Another concrete wall. Why boy?

After a moment he said, "Faith, you've had a hard time. Living on the streets. Getting hammered on the head. I don't know what brought you to the streets originally. God knows you sound educated. But whatever it was, you're suffering from some, I don't know, obsession. Delusion even. Guy North tells me you act dazed sometimes, half asleep. I looked it up on the Web. You may have dissociative fugue."

"It sounds like something I was supposed to learn to play on the piano." (Since when did I know that I had once played piano?)

"It's a psychiatric disorder which can be brought on by trauma. And now you're seeing evidence of foul play where there is no evidence. If a kid was wandering around alone, wouldn't someone have reported him missing?"

"Maybe he was deliberately abandoned. Maybe something incomprehensible happened. Why are you and Guy North so negative about everything?"

"Negative!" He clutched his handsome grizzled head in mock despair.

"Didn't you just tell me how kind we were? Didn't I drive right out at the drop of your voice? Aren't we doing our damnedest – "

"No responsible adult would allow a child to dig up someone else's perfect garden."

"Maybe this kid was being taken care of by a bigger kid. You know, like an irresponsible ten year old. Or maybe the mother was inside the house chatting with the owner and the kid was playing outside alone. I can think of a dozen possibilities."

"Lieutenant – Augie – would you mind if we talked to some neighbors?"

Amenably, he motioned me back to the car and we went east along Pepper Ridge for about a quarter of a mile before we came to the next house. It was a converted farmhouse, a two story gray clapboard which had been gentrified. A white haired woman in her sixties opened the door. Her face was toughened and burnished by the outdoors and her body was muscular. She wore tight black stretch pants and a loose knitted black pullover.

"Ma'am, I'm a police officer," Augie said, showing her his ID. "Do you know the Buitenkamps?"

Agitated, she said, "Nothing's happened to Claire, has it?"

"No, Ma'am, it's nothing like that. We just want to locate her."

"Why? Was the house broken into?"

"This lady has some business with her and since she isn't home we thought a neighbor might know where she is."

"She's out of town. Visiting her sister in Buffalo."

"Does she have children or grandchildren?"

"No, she's a childless widow. What's this all about?"

"Do you know how we can get in touch with her?"

"No, I don't have her sister's address."

"Well, no hurry. Thank you, Ma'am."

Before she could shut the door I said, "Mrs. Uh – do you know of any children living on this road?"

"Children? Why do you want to know?"

"It's sort of complicated. If you could just tell us – "

"Yes. There are some teens up the road – I'm not sure of their names – and one little boy down at the other end – "

"On the other side of the Buitenkamps?"

"Yes. If you would tell me – "

"Thanks Mrs. uh – thank you."

I took the lieutenant's arm and pulled him back to the car, "Lieutenant – uh Augie – one more stop. Let's go to the house past Claire Buitencamp's."

"Sure."

In the car I said, "Augie, you have any children?"

"I'm divorced. No children."

"If you had children you'd understand why I'm concerned about a child possibly wandering around alone – "

"I *would* be concerned if that's what I thought was going on. You know something Faith?"

A car speeded past us. "They oughtn't to drive so fast on a road with children," I said.

"You look different."

"Guy North gave me some clothes from his store."

He turned left at the next driveway past the Buitencamp house and we climbed slowly past oaks and sugar maples. I caught a glimpse through the trees of a long rambling one story brick house with a Jeep Wagoneer parked in front.

"I'm not talking about clothes. It's something else. Your expression. You seem more – I don't know what to call it – more *awake* as if – " A beeper went off. "Shit. I have to find a telephone."

"Don't policemen use radios or cell phones or something?"

"The uniformed guys do. But there are dead spots so I still use a beeper. Could I take you back to Guy North's house and use the telephone there?"

I nodded and decided that I could walk back here after I let Augie use the phone. He turned to back down the drive, placing his arm along the back of his seat so that his finger tips just grazed my shoulder. His driving was excellent and I felt a childish tingle of pleasure about being in a car with this handsome, competent man. Added to it was the pleasure of being taken care of that I had also felt in Guy's house. Perhaps not very politically correct for a woman in the Twenty-first Century, but after living on the streets for God knew how long, I was ready for a little dependency. We drove back to Route 120 and turned left on Water Wheel Road.

At Guy North's house, I unlocked the door and waved Augie towards the telephone. I went to the kitchen to get a glass of water. I could hear him saying, "Augie Gunther . . . Yeah . . . Okay . . . On my way."

"Got to go," he told me. Then he hesitated, almost embarrassed. Finally he said, "Would you like to see a movie tonight?"

"What?"

"There's a movie I've been wanting to see – the Prairie Home Companion thing – and I don't have anybody else to ask right now and I hate going alone – "

"You're asking *me* to go to a movie with you?"

"I didn't think this would be such a tough concept for you to grasp. Why not?"

"Well, this will be my second date in two days after, who knows, maybe decades of, well, datelessness . . . So, why?"

"I just told you. Also, I need to keep you off the streets."

"You must know a dozen women who'd go to a movie with you."

"Not at this moment. Besides, I'm like Guy North. I pick up strays. Hey, I've got to get to work. I'll check with you later."

I went to the window to watch him drive off. When he was gone, I examined myself in the bathroom mirror. The stranger reflected there had dry rough skin, lines around her eyes and mouth, innocuous features. Also, although the fact didn't register in this particular small mirror, a thin and out of shape figure. On the other hand, even I could see that this person had once been attractive, maybe even lovely.

But why was the handsome lieutenant asking me for a date? To distract me from my purpose? Ever since I'd mentioned the house on Salmon Kill, both he and Guy North had been behaving strangely. As if protecting me. Protecting me from what?

I checked the kitchen clock. Only ten in the morning. I had to get back to the house that I had glimpsed on Pepper Ridge. But first, I needed a few minutes to calm down and think. I made a cup of tea and sat down at the table. Perhaps because of my encounter with Conrad Van Kuhn earlier, I thought back to my visit to the newspaper office. I seemed to be watching the microfilm whir by in my head: Judge brought up on ethics charge; recycling drive coordinated among the villages of South Springport Township; conflict managing training sessions for district administrators; meeting of the local historical society to discuss better record keeping; local boy finishing second –

Meeting of the historical society to discuss better record keeping.

I consulted the local telephone book. South Springport Courthouse and Museum. South Springport Historical Society. I tried the latter. No answer. Then the museum with the same result. A museum not open on a Saturday in June? Maybe the library would have the name I needed. Miraculously, someone at the library answered.

"Don't tell me you're open!" I exclaimed.

An amused voice. "From ten to one on Saturday."

"I need some information but the Historical Society is closed – "

"Ten to two on Mondays, Wednesdays and Fridays."

"Do you by any chance know the name of the town historian?" (How did I know there was one?)

"Becky Schnell."

"Would you spell it please?"

"S-c-h-n-e-l-l."

"She in the local directory?"

"Sure thing."

"Thank you."

Only one Schnell, not Becky but William. A woman answered.

"Mrs. Schnell?"

"That's me."

"Are you Becky Schnell, the town historian?"

"Among other things."

A woman who answered like that couldn't be all bad. I nearly asked her about the other things but, restraining myself, said, "Mrs. Schnell, I have an odd request."

"Odd requests are my specialty."

No point in beating about the bush then.

"I'm suffering from memory loss. I've just returned to South Springport after – uh – some time and I found someone else living in my house. If I could get into the tax assessor's office I might find my name among the former owners – "

"It'll open Monday."

Quirky she might be, but how would she react to a statement like, "I need the answer now. It's a matter of life and death"?

"I'm aware of that but for certain reasons I'd like the answer before Monday."

"What can *I* do?"

"You're the town historian. You might know more than most people about who lived in which house when."

"Only if they're historical. On the other hand, it *is* a small town and I've lived here all my life. Which house is it?"

"One forty Salmon Kill. The brick house."

I waited. Nothing happened. Had she hung up? Had we been disconnected?

"Mrs. Schnell?"

"You say you once lived in that house?"

"Yes."

"When – why did you leave?"

"That's just it. I don't know."

"What's your name?"

"That's what I'm trying to find out."

"Oh yes, of course. I'm not – where have you been living in the meantime?"

"On the streets."

"The streets? Which streets?"

"Mrs. Schnell, have you any idea who used to live in that house before the Cushmans and the Bossicas?"

"If you lost your memory how did you happen to come to South Springport?"

"My memory is erratic. I get flashes of – oh – light and then I'm back in the dark again."

"Why don't you go to the police?"

"I have. They say wait until the tax assessor office opens Monday."

"Where are you now?"

"I'm at Guy North's house. Do you know him?"

"Can't *he* help you? How do you happen to be in his house?"

"He says wait until Monday."

"And you don't want to."

I no longer knew what to say.

Silence again and then, "Ok, come to my house."

"Your house? Why?"

"The tax assessor is my cousin. She'll open the office for us. "

Something in her voice was making my stomach churn. It was like having an official appear on your doorstep and say, "Are you the Mrs. So and So whose husband was driving a blue station wagon this morning – " I wanted to hang up and run. Escape from South Springport and return to the park bench. I felt as if I had been swallowing bits of straw for years and they had wadded into an impossible lump within me.

"Okay, I'll get a cab and go to, where?"

"You don't have a car? I'll pick you up. "

TWENTY

Saturday, June 9
Dilly

A ant crawling on Mommy's face. I shooed it but I didn't kill it. Dr. Ribaudo fix you, Mommy. How you doing? You be happy soon? How I call Dr. Ribaudo? I know how to make a R. When I grow up, be a big kid, I fix you.

A big deer and a little deer eating Mommy's patience. I yelled, "Don't eat it." They didn't listen. I remembered. Be quiet. Was the Man in the house? Baby deer drink from bottles? I went to look. Sir still in the pool. I throwed a stick. "Fetch," I said. He didn't. I goed around to see if the Man's car in the driveway. No car. I opened a French door. It was the study. How many days Mommy not home? I holded up all my fingers. We used to build bridges with Legos. Mommy did most. Sometimes she putted a blanket from the chair to the book shelf. We pretended bad guys attacking. We were in the tent and shooted at them. I shooted Mommy. She falled over dead. She didn't mind. I don't have much enemies. I might write Chris to visit. He can sleep on the floor. I miss him actually. We could have a discussion.

I pushed the stool to the counter and washed a bottle. I wished I had juice. I filled the bottle with water. The nipple didn't go on. I drinked from the bottle. I got grapes and cheese from the refrigerator. I eated on the floor. They didn't taste much. Grapes good for you? Make you grow? I lied on the floor and looked out the window to the clouds. It was beautiful.

The house was growing garbage. Mommy wouldn't like it when she waked up. I went to the telephone and dialed 0. Some lady answered. I said, "Come here, please." The dial comed on. I putted the telephone back. Why lady hanged up? Why Mommy sick? Why Man comed here?

I hopped on one foot. I nearly falled but I grabbed a chair. When Mommy taked business trips and leaved me with Cindy, she holded up her fingers. "I be back in five days. Cross days on calendar. I bring you a tractor." Sometimes I want to go. She can't take me. Business trip. Mommy writes contracts. She taked me to Carbeen. That's a island. Last time I had my own seat. The cake was horrible. When we got out it was hot. Then we taked a little plane. No food. Mommy said look down. The water was green. The little white dots were sailboats. Tan was sand. It was summer when we went down the stairs on the plane. Mommy said it was snowing at home. Mommy's friend hugged me.

We taked a motorboat to the island. I weared a life jacket.

The Jeep was the best part. It climbed way up. I seed snakes and lizards. Mommy said look at the scenery. She was bothering my idea. Always telling me look. The house had a roof but no walls. Well, some walls, but not much. The lizards comed into the house. They were my pets. I named them but I couldn't tell which was Sally and which was Tina.

I eated a mango. It was delicious. I wished I had one now. It sticked in my teeth.

I'm bored of being alone. Where Tracy live? Have to go by car. Maybe Mommy come home today. I forgot. Really forgot. Mommy home already. Asleep. I practiced days. Sunday, Monday, Wednesday, Saturday, Monday. Mommy says practice. One two three four five six eight nine eleven fifteen. In the Carbeen Mommy put flippers on her feet and snorkeled. That means looking at things. I was too little. I stayed in the boat and watched. She bringed me shells. Also a sea fan. It waved in water. She couldn't catch a fish. You know what comes from the west? Storms. Also cowboys. Did Mommy water plants? It was worrying me. I taked the stool to the sink and putted water in the can. Not too much. It was heavy. Some spilled. I watered the plants. Mommy be proud of me.

I don't like the Man. I won't talk to him. I'll ignore him. I feeled grumpy. I wanted to go to the Familiar Drummer. Order French fries. Also a chocolate pop. Bad for cavities. A little bit okay. Maybe I could visit Mrs. B. again. She home yet? She hugs a lot. She always has ice cream. This is really bothering me. I want Mommy wake up. The house is a mess. Soon she wake up. I help her clean. Do her a favor. Maybe I won't be bad again. Never. Ever. I went to my room to draw. I like drawing. When I grow up I be a truck driver.

Somebody yelled, "Lorraine!" That's Mommy's name.

I yelled back, "Susie! Susie! Susie!" maybe eighteen times. Susie is Mommy's friend. I knowed her voice. I runned to the front door. Susie was waiting behind the glass. I turned the knob and the button popped out. I jumped on Susie. I holded on to her pants. I couldn't stop crying. She picked me up. I holded her neck. She said, "Dilly, what's going on?" She looked. She goed to the kitchen. She called Lorraine and she runned through the house. She said, "My God." I said, "Mommy hurt herself." She said, "Where she is?" I said, "In the barn."

She grabbed my hand so hard it hurted. I didn't mind. She was a fast runner. I had to run fast. I said, "Be careful. Don't fall in the pool." She didn't. She saw Sir. I said, "Why you crying Susie?" Susie didn't pay 'tention. Susie runned into the barn and bended over Mommy. She pushed the boat away. She pulled Mommy out. She putted her hand on Mommy's neck and she tried to open Mommy's eyes. Then she standed.

"Come on," she said. "We have to go for help."

I asked, Mommy dead? Susie said no.

I seed something. I didn't know what. It moved. A big shadow. The Man. "Look out, Suzie!" I yelled. The Man had a thing in his hand. He zoomed on Susie's head. I cried. "You hurted Susie!" He hurted Susie again and I yelled. He pushed Susie on the floor next to Mommy. He throwed the horse blanket on them. I cried. "They can't breathe." He didn't care. He grabbed and it hurted me. I tried to kick. He said, "Dilly, waiting time over. Feeding time here."

SKIP

The boss invited Father to go sailing and he said bring your son. I'd lived my entire life in Maine and I'd never been on anything bigger than a rowboat. The boat wasn't fancy like the boats on TV but it was pretty neat. It had two bedrooms called staterooms and two toilets called heads and a kitchen called a galley and a living room called a salon. On boats everything has a different name.

It was a lot of work getting started. First you take plastic covers off things like the compass and the instrument panel and then you unlock the downstairs, only it isn't called the downstairs, and you bring up pillows and stuff for sitting. The boss studied maps – he called them charts – like he was planning a trip around the world. Even starting the engine for getting away from the dock was a big deal. Father had to do something called "cast off" and he nearly fell into the water trying to get back on the boat. He got tangled in the ropes – they're called lines – just trying to get back on the boat. The boss yelled, "Bring in the fenders" and Father nearly lost one of them. Then the boss said to put the fenders in the lazaret and I nearly laughed watching Father trying to decide what the lazaret was. "Back there, behind you," the boss said and then he told Father to get the pennant. Father always liked to look like he knew what he was doing but he didn't know shit.

"Time to put up the sails," the boss said. To hear him say it, you would think it was the greatest treat in the world. He yelled things like "Clear the sheet. Get the handle" and then he pushed Father out of the way and said, "You do it, Skip." I didn't look at Father. At first I thought I'd pretend I was useless so Father wouldn't get mad, but I couldn't stop myself. I loosened the rope on one side and then turned the winch handle on the other side as hard as I could and the mainsail came blowing out. It was fun. The boss said, "Great, Skip. Now the jib." I worked up a sweat and the boss said, "You sure could teach your old man a thing or two."

Soon I would.

When the sails were up, the boss said, "Watch carefully, Skip. The way you turn the engine off is you pull this knob out and then push it back before you cut the engine." He ignored Father and Father was getting madder and madder.

It was sunny, but when we got away from the land it was cold. It was early June. I hadn't brought a sweater and the boss gave me a slicker. Father said he didn't need one. He tried to look like he was enjoying himself but he was starting to look sick. I hoped he wouldn't throw up because first of all, it would make him even madder, and second of all, I'd be the one who had to clean it up.

"Trim the sails," the boss said and showed me how to pull in the sheet around the winch clockwise and pass it over what he called the feed and the sheave and clinch it. I was learning a lot. The boss was as happy as a kid and kept saying, "Perfect day. Isn't this great? I told you you'd love it."

Then he told Father to take the wheel and keep to one twenty. Father said, "You know, Harold, I've never sailed before." The boss said there was nothing to it. "If you know how to drive a car, you can sail a boat." Then he went down what he called the companion way and sat down at what he called his nav table. Now and then he yelled things like "Head up." "What's head up?" Father yelled back. "Turn into the wind." Father didn't know what he was talking about. I didn't either. Father turned the wheel and I thought for sure the boat would capsize. It scared me. We were a long way from shore and the water was cold.

"The other way," the boss yelled and the boat straightened out. Father's lips were blue and the tip of his nose was white and he had red eyes. He looked like the American flag. He kept turning the wheel back and forth and the sails made a lot of noise flapping in the wind and did what the boss called luffing. I wished the boss would come up but he was charting a course he said. He had the radio on and it made a racket the whole time, people talking to each other about "I'll see you tonight at the mussel shack" or "Get back to the marina and pick up the groceries." It didn't sound like the movies. And Father didn't look like one of those movie captains with his head thrown back and his shoulders tall and straight. Instead, he was hunched over the wheel and his knuckles on the wheel were white from holding on so tight. The boat began to tip over again with the rail almost in the water and Father yelled, "Harold!" but what with the wind and the radio, the boss didn't hear him. I was worried. Father didn't know what he was doing. It seemed to me that if the rail went in the water when you turned one way, you ought to turn the other way. I looked back at father's hands and he caught me looking and I could tell he was planning what he was going to do to me when we got home.

The boss called out he was going to the head and to keep to the course. We could hardly hear him above the racket from the radio. Some guy saying, "This is Victory calling Robin," and a girl saying, "This is Robin, Victory" and the guy saying, "Robin, switch to channel 86. Over."

The boat began to tip over again and I yelled without thinking, "Father, turn the wheel." He looked daggers at me and gave the wheel a shove and said, "You do it, you're so smart." Then he stepped out of the cockpit onto the deck. The boat was tipping over again and the deck was wet and slippery. He was right next to what the boss called the life lines.

All of a sudden it hit me. Now or never. It was in my hands. The only hands that would ever help me.

I grabbed Father's shoulders and he was so surprised he didn't even get a chance to yell before I pushed him hard. He grabbed the life lines and went straight over the side, hanging on. His face was purple and he yelled but I was sure the boss couldn't hear him with the wind and the radio and him being in the head. I got the winch handle from its pocket and smashed Father's knuckles as hard as I could. And then he was gone.

Even when he was gone I could still see his eyes, big and scared and his mouth open, like the way I looked, I guess, when he was doing what he did to me.

The boat was out of control. The sails and lines were snapping like whips. Father wasn't a good swimmer. How long could he last? The water was pretty rough and the wind strong. The boss said the water temperature might be about forty or fifty degrees. I tried to hold the wheel steady. How long before the boss would come up? I couldn't see any sign of Father. Only the colored lobster pots. I looked at the compass. I tried to remember the course but I couldn't. The numbers kept swinging back and forth. I had to pick the exact right time to call the boss. Not so soon Father might be saved. Not so late the boss would come up and find him missing.

I heard a pumping noise. He was flushing the toilet.

"Mr. Bernstein!" I yelled. I tried to sound scared. I was. "Mr. Bernstein!"

Nothing happened. He couldn't hear me. Suddenly the boom went crashing to the other side. If I'd been a couple of inches taller I'd have had my head knocked off. I yelled louder.

The boss came running up. "What's going on?" he said. "Jesus. You jibed." He began loosening one line, pulling in the other.

"Mr. Bernstein!" I yelled. "Father went overboard!"

I thought he would have a fit. "Here, grab this," he yelled, throwing me a rope. I never saw anybody move so fast. He began throwing things off the boat. A life preserver, a flashing light, a pole with a flag on top. Then he started taking the sails down. He kept yelling directions at me and the boom went crashing over my head again. I tried to help but he kept pushing me out of the way and doing most of it all by himself. When the sails were wrapped up he turned the motor on and headed back to where he'd dropped the preserver and the light and the pole. I didn't see Father. "Go below and call the Coast Guard," the boss yelled at me.

"How?" I said.

"Turn the radio to channel sixteen – " Then he said never mind and told me to circle the preserver and not run over Father. He handed me the wheel. I kept looking for Father so I could run over him but everything in the water looked the same.

I didn't even care if I was arrested. Jail would be better than Father any day.

I could hear the boss yelling downstairs, "Mayday, Mayday, Mayday. Man overboard. Man overboard. Man overboard. This is the vessel Eluria." Then a lot of stuff about our position. So many degrees North and something else East of East Chebeague Island. "A man fell overboard about ten minutes ago and we cannot locate him. Our vessel is a white forty-two foot sloop. Mayday, Mayday, Mayday. Please come in, Coast Guard."

And then a man answered almost right away. "Eluria, this is the Coast Guard and we are about twelve minutes away from your vessel. Do not leave your current position. Keep circling and looking for the swimmer. Repeat. Keep circling and we'll be there in twelve minutes."

The boss ran downstairs and came running back up with binoculars and told me to keep looking while he handled the boat. I looked through the binoculars and focused them but all I could see was water. I couldn't keep them steady. I tried to look worried and I kept wiping my eyes as if I were crying,

"There it is!" the boss yelled.

I nearly fainted, thinking he meant Father. But it was the Coast Guard. A slick white boat came racing towards us. It slowed down and two men got into a smaller boat and they began circling the floating life preserver and the other stuff we'd thrown into the water. There was a lot of shouting back and forth between the boss and the Coast Guard and radios blasting. It seemed to go on forever. I don't know how much time passed. But after a while I relaxed. Father had to be dead by now.

TWENTY-ONE

Saturday, June 9
Faith

Becky Schnell, the town historian, was a large woman in her fifties with dark hair that was cut for convenience rather than for style, and a face molded for practicality rather than for beauty. She wore a beige rayon blouse and a sand colored skirt decorated with a map of some tourist attraction. In a pleasant, educated voice, she introduced herself and then said, "My cousin, the tax assessor" – she smiled uneasily – "will meet us at the Town Hall."

As we headed for her car, a fancy white Acura, it seemed to me she was on tenterhooks as much as I was. It was as if we were off on some grim errand having to do with business or maybe to visit someone who was very ill at the hospital.

I was so distracted, I forgot to lock Guy North's door or take the key. It was clear outdoors, the sky unbelievably blue, and the trees post card green. It looked the way that God might have imagined the world should look, if God were truly benevolent. I had the beginning of a head and chest ache. The dazzling clarity of the universe hurt my eyes and I felt out of place as if this world were simply too beautiful for someone like me.

"It's kind of you to go to all this trouble for a stranger," I said formally as if she'd wrangled me an invitation to a posh party. Was it kind? Or . . . the only other word that occurred to me was cruel.

"Why is it so important for you get the information today rather than wait for Monday?"

Everyone funneling down into the same narrow channel. My mind seemed to be leaking clarity of thought. This was probably how the expression "mind like a sieve" came into being. "I have this inexplicable sense of urgency – " The sentence leaked away also, and to fill the silence, I said, "This is such a warm, friendly town. Everyone has tried to help."

"I don't think South Springport is unusual that way. Wouldn't *you* try to help someone in trouble? Particularly if it didn't take any great sacrifice on your part? Didn't you ever give money to charity?"

I remembered, as if in the distant past, the handicapped Vietnam veteran. I almost laughed out loud. Then I was distracted by the fact that she was driving slowly, apparently in no hurry to reach the Town Hall.

In addition, she'd turned the wrong way, heading towards Freeport.

"You taking the scenic route?" I asked in what was meant to be a light hearted tone.

"My cousin will be slightly delayed and I thought we'd drive around a bit. Maybe shake loose a few memories for you."

We drove through Freeport – it was too early in the season for the crowds – turned right on Bow Street and drove a few more miles. I was surprised by how quickly the stores fell away and we were on a pretty country road. Then we were approaching a narrow causeway, crossing what looked to be a tidal river. Fields opened up on either side and to the left was a picture perfect farm. Too good to be true. And in fact it was. A sign announced that we were entering a pretend farm. Wolfe's Neck Farm. Recompence Shore Campsites. I looked to the right and across the field, I glimpsed the ocean, flat and calm as a lake. I closed my eyes.

Not only was something shaking loose, something was *crawling* inside of me.

"What's wrong?" she asked sharply.

I had dropped my head so that my chin touched my chest and I crossed my arms protectively over my chest. I didn't look up or open my eyes but I knew exactly what I would see – a long dirt road to my right that meandered along the shore, through fields and woodlands, past dozens of shoreline campsites. As she started to make the right turn, something snapped. "No!" I shouted.

The car stopped. "No?"

"I don't want to go there."

"Why not?" Her voice was flat.

"I really don't feel – I'm afraid we'll be keeping your cousin waiting."

I felt her looking at me for a long minute but I kept my eyes on my lap. I was afraid that if she asked me any questions, I might . . . I didn't know what. Scream? Cry? I just wanted to be gone from that place.

"Ok." She said finally and turned the car around. We drove back to Freeport, neither of us speaking and headed west to South Springport. When we reached Route 120, we turned right and passed the little church where Mrs. Lamonagne had thought she had recognized me and then decided she had not. We left behind the neighborhood of tidy houses fronted by pretty gardens and parked in the driveway in front of the Town Hall. Since it was Saturday, there was only one car parked there – presumably the cousin's.

Tossing her shoulder strap purse over her arm, Becky Schnell went up the steps and headed down the corridor to the office with TAX ASSESSOR lettered in black on frosted glass. I followed reluctantly. Inside a woman waited for us, also middle-aged but petite and harried looking. She was dressed in wrinkled jeans and a gray sweatshirt. Clearly the less prosperous, or at least, less self-conscious branch of the family. She nodded at Becky, it seemed to me, in a conspiratorial manner.

At the back of the room were two desks and chairs, but the rest of the room was filled with rows of cabinets, chest high, with long sliding drawers.

"The house you're interested in is 140 Salmon Kill, right?" Becky Schnell said to me. She seemed to have metamorphosed from a sympathetic bystander to a stiff bureaucrat. In fact, she seemed to be having trouble breathing. Moreover, she had apparently left behind any vestige of her suburban manner and failed to introduce me to the cousin. The cousin turned to her computer and spent some minutes clicking away. Then she motioned to me to come around and look at the computer screen. Through a haze I saw parcels 191.71-6-2 and 191.71-6-3 with an acreage of six point two and then a series of land values: one hundred and ten thousand, two hundred and fifty-five thousand, four hundred and eighty thousand. The purchase price sky rocketing with each new owner.

"Does the name Unger mean anything to you?" the cousin asked.

I felt nauseated. The room revolved around me as if I were caught in a slow moving tornado. Gently, someone took my hand and pushed me into a chair. I'd learned how to circumvent the pitfalls on the Boston streets: avoid knots of teenagers clustered on street corners; don't go near certain subway stops late at night; don't count your money in public; keep away from the weirdos, loonies and thugs. For some people, *I* was the pitfall, the person to be avoided. South Springport, on the other hand, was populated by do gooders who took care of strangers; it was a paradise of rolling hills and woodlands; it was dotted with establishments bearing cutesy names like The Familiar Drummer and The Clip Joint. It had white steepled and stone New England churches and many acres of nearby protected parks and seashore.

South Springport was a stretch of waving grasses concealing a stinking swamp underneath. One misstep and you sank into suffocating, oozing slime.

"Is that your name?" someone was asking. I had nearly forgotten Becky Schnell and her accommodating, nameless cousin.

"What happened to . . . uh, Faith?" I asked in a hoarse quavering voice. A voice I hardly recognized. I could not bring myself to say the second name.

The woman's face weaved and swirled as if under water. "She disappeared."

"And – "

"She was never found."

"Didn't – weren't inquiries made?"

"Of course. But she was a divorcee. Her ex-husband had gone to New Zealand. No siblings. Her parents were dead of some disease they contracted while on a safari in Africa. The police were finally able to trace a cousin living out West. He came to town to take care of the – uh – legalities, and after a time, inherited the estate, I guess. He must have sold the house to the Bossicas."

I found myself being led back to the car by Becky Schnell while her cousin remained behind to lock up.

"Where are we going?"

"Where would you like to go?"

"I don't know," I said and I meant it. Whistles, sirens, bells were going off inside my head. Blinking lights warned of a catastrophic meltdown. The ground swayed or maybe I did.

Without knowing how I had arrived there, I found myself back at Guy North's house.

"Lie down," Becky Schnell said. "Is there brandy in the house?"

"You want a drink?" I asked stupidly.

"It's for you."

"I don't want it."

She led me to the sofa. "Why don't you try to relax?"

"Was she – was Faith living alone at the time she disappeared?"

"There's plenty of time to go into all of that later."

The words "plenty of time" made me struggle to get up. "No! That's just it! There is no time!"

"How can you say that when so much time has already passed?"

"Now that I have a name I want to go back to the newspaper office and look it up."

"I'm afraid I can't take the responsibility – "

"What are you talking about? You're not taking the responsibility for anything. I'm grateful for what you did. Now I'm going to take a cab – "

"You can't go off alone." She placed a restraining hand on my arm. "Tell you what. If you sit here a minute and let me make a couple of phone calls

I'll drive you to the newspaper office."

"Phone calls to whom?"

"Oh, you know. The newspaper office to tell them we're on our way. Is there a telephone in the kitchen?"

"Yes." I sat down again. Caught in a net of wanting to advance and wanting to retreat, I didn't try to overhear her conversation. Besides, her words were mumbled. Evidently she had gone to the other end of the kitchen and turned her back. I was reminded of my childhood, listening to my mother explaining my chicken pox symptoms to the doctor. It was oddly soothing. Leave it to the grownups.

"Let's go," she said, "the newspaper office said it was okay to come over."

"You made more than one call."

She was beginning to look faintly disordered from running her fingers repeatedly through her hair. Clearly, she wasn't used to this kind of thing. Finally, she said, "I called the police."

"The police?"

"Well, it's their bailiwick, isn't it? You're a missing person. And if you really *are* this Faith Unger, there are bound to be a lot of legalities – of course you're not sure you are Faith Unger, are you?"

Was I? I wasn't sure of anything. Least of all if I *wanted* to be Faith Unger. "Are the police coming here?"

"No, they'll meet us at the newspaper office."

"Whom else did you call?"

"What?"

"I thought I heard you dialing three times."

"Oh – my daughter. To tell her where I was." She was lying and this was something else she wasn't used to. Why was she in this overwrought state? Simply an historian's interest in town events? Compassion? The rubber necking instinct for inspecting mutilated bodies and dazed survivors?

South Springport's landmarks were becoming increasingly familiar, but I couldn't separate impressions of the last forty-eight hours from possible long ago memories. We passed a restaurant I might have dined in. A pre-school nursery. Past and present were fusing. The Springport Express seemed different. During my last visit, no one had shown any interest in me, but now it seemed to me that clusters of people stopped talking to watch us go by. The girl at the reception desk waved us on into the so-called library without inquiring about our business, although she too scrutinized me closely. One thing was certain – I was no long invisible.

I spotted Conrad at the far end of the room. He was standing with his hands in his pockets. He looked nervous and I saw that it wasn't deadline pressure that was making him nervous this time. It was me. I noticed another a man who, for some reason, I was sure did not belong in a newspaper office. For one thing he was older than the others, in his late sixties, and for another, he was wearing a business suit and tie as opposed to casual sport clothes. Leaning against the wall, he appeared to be trying to keep out of the way, remain invisible, while at the same time inspecting me closely as if searching for symptoms imperceptible to mere laymen. And then I knew what he was and to whom Becky Schnell had made her third call.

Someone offered me coffee, which I declined, and someone else spread out a large leather bound ledger on a table. Wetting an index finger, the latter flipped through the newsprint. Now and then he glanced up at me and then at the man who didn't belong. Finally, having found what he was searching for, he straightened. At the same moment a flashbulb popped. "That's intolerable," Becky Schnell protested, and the woman standing beside Conrad who had aimed the camera at me, retorted, "That's the newspaper business."

An expanding lump in my throat threatened to choke me. Somewhere inside my head was a memory of me saying, "I've changed my mind," and a laughing nurse telling me, "It's too late. The baby is almost here."

Too late. Forces beyond my control were barreling me along and nothing could stop them. I had started the machinery and the machinery would produce what it was programmed to produce. Impassable barriers had sprung up behind me, making retreat impossible. The only escape was suicide and how did one commit suicide in a crowded room without weapons, without high windows? Trapped, looking from face to face – the man in the business suit, the photographer, reporters, editors, a possible plainclothesman, a stricken Becky Schnell – I was reminded of a dentist who had held a drill behind him while smiling into my childish eyes and saying, "It'll only hurt a little."

"What did you find?" I asked faintly, but I knew the answer. Some part of me had known all along. Which was why I had hidden behind those layers of forgetfulness all those years. But now the tattered pieces were being stripped away, leaving me naked and exposed to the truth.

I approached the table and looked down. At first all I saw was a confused mélange of black and white which could have been Chinese for all the sense it made to me. Or I could have been suffering from a mental illness which made it impossible to understand the written word. I blinked, forcing myself to focus.

BODY OF MISSING THREE OLD FOUND!
"FLY" KILLER STRIKES AGAIN

Monday, June 10. The body of three-year-old Bobby Unger of Salmon Kill Road was discovered at Wolfe's Neck Recompense Camping Ground late last night by a posse composed of local and state police. A dead fly was pinned to the boy's chest, recalling the still unsolved murder in 1980 of four year old William Senio. Police were led to the scene of the crime by four year old Theodore Haskell of Lake Drive. Theodore and Bobby had been taken on an overnight camping trip on Friday by Bobby's mother, Mrs. Faith Unger. When Mrs. Unger and the two boys failed to return on Saturday morning, Mrs. Joan Haskell, mother of Theodore, first instigated a search of her own and then informed the police. It wasn't until nearly midnight last night that the police found Theodore, in a state of shock, as he recounted the events of Friday evening. According to the boy, a "monster" entered the tent after the three of them were asleep Friday evening, tied up Mrs. Unger and attacked Bobby. While the murderer was occupied with the other two, Theodore managed to escape and wandered, terrified, forty-eight hours before being rescued. Police were unable to locate Mrs. Unger. The condition of the three-year-old's body, similar to that of the Senio child, was such that one police officer fainted and another became sick. The boy had been—

I started to scream, a long, blistering, ear splitting shriek, and then I felt a sharp jab in my arm. The man who didn't belong was holding a hypodermic needle and wrapping his arms around me – either to keep me from falling or from striking out. Voices rose in a tumultuous bedlam and then darkness encompassed me and I fell into a deep welcoming pit of nothingness.

TWENTY-TWO

Saturday, June 9
Dilly

I told the man, "You killed Susie! You killed Mommy!" I wasn't brave. I cried. He didn't talk. All he did was, he looked. "I don't have much enemies," I said. "You a enemy."

Susie had blood coming from her head. She didn't move. Mommy didn't move. Why the Man not talk? Why he not say he sorry?

He hitted me on the face and I falled. Nobody hitted me before. Ever. I tried to suck air. It didn't go in. Like in the pool. I hated it. Sometimes Tracy push me. Once Chris throwed a truck and it hitted me in the stomach. This was worse. The Man wasn't like when he babysitted me. I hated him. I was more scared than when I was alone. I said, "I want my Mommy." He said, "You be with her soon." I said, "When?" He said, "Soon." I said, "I wanna' snuggle her now." He said, "She not really here. She some place else." I said, "You fooling me, right?" He said, "Go in the house."

I didn't want to. I yelled, "It's not the rules!" I runned to the woods. He taked my foot and dragged me to the house. I bumped my head. I cried. I begged him let me go. He didn't.

He said, "Now the fun begins."

I said, "This is no fun!"

He said did I remember the story about the fly. I said I forget. He said he had fun with kids my age. I said, "Who? Chris? Tracy?" He said who Chris, who Tracy? He said maybe he could have fun with them. He said, "They live alone with mommies? They have daddies?" I said they have daddies. He said he never have fun when kids have daddies. He said, "Know what happens kids are bad?" I said I not bad. He told me. I was scared. Maybe he teasing. I didn't believe it. I said, "Where your father is?" He said, "Fathoms five." I said, "What that mean?" He said, "Father in the water." I said, "How?" He said, "Boating accident." "Where your mommy?" I said. "She goed away, like your mommy," he said. "She coming back?" I said. He said no.

He pulled me up the stairs to my room. He putted on the light in my room. The mirror Uncle Moore gived me laughed.

The Man not brave. He yelled, "Who there?" I almost telled him about the mirror, but I didn't. I said, "Uncle Moore." I was teasing. The Man letted me go. He runned to look. I runned down the stairs, out the house to the woods and up the ladder to the tree house.

The Man comed out. He didn't know where I was. He said bad words. Also what he do to me. I hided under the blue plastic roof. I didn't listen. I holded my ears. I wait maybe a hour or maybe some minutes. I listened. No Man. Maybe Man come here. I climbed down. I'm a good climber. I runned in the woods. I always beat Mommy when we run. Get on mark, get ready, go. I didn't stop to see Mommy and Susie in the barn. The woods are big. Anybody can hide. Get lost even. Once I fooled Mommy and she got scared she couldn't find me. Branches scratched. I didn't care. I didn't go on paths. I runned through the scratchy woods. I hided behind the stone wall. I listened. No Man. He hiding? I made no noise. I runned some more. I seed the stream. If my feet get wet, he can track me like Indians. I comed to a stone wall. Mommy said in olden days the walls showed where the farms are. I hided deep under leaves. I was buried. I hided every part. I hardly breathed, Was poison ivy? I didn't care. Poison ivy better than Man. Once I heared crashing. Far away. I breathed under the leaves. How many hours? I don't know. No more crashing. Man playing a trick? What I should do? Wait for night time and peek? No more going home.

It's dangerous. Stay in woods. What I eat? No berries like in Hansel and Gretel. I wished I had a magic lamp. What I wish? Lobster. Steak even. Wish Mommy wake up. Maybe I cross the stream? Find somebody nice? I peeked. No Man. I holded up my fingers.

Five hours. I went to the stream. I finded the log to cross the stream. I wrapped my hands and knees around the log. Mommy says, "Wish you hugged me like a log." The log was slippery. I holded on tight and crawled. Like a baby but I'm not a baby. I got to the other side. I was all muddy.

Can Mommy find me this side? "Mommy, come here!" I listened. No answer. Mommy maybe dead. Mrs. B. adopt me? Maybe Uncle Moore. Geoff and Peg maybe. What's adopt? You baby sit somebody not your kid. I want Mommy adopt me. I rubbed some mud off. I wished I had strawberries. Sometimes Mommy and I find raspberries. Mommy saved some. I eated mine. Mommy planted vegetables in the garden. I helped. Were they growed? I could go to the garden night time and eat vegetables. The Man wouldn't see. Lettuce and beans. Mrs. B. have a vegetable garden? She didn't care if I taked some. It wasn't stealing. If she home she'd give me ice cream. She says, "Don't tell Mommy." Man know where Mrs. B. live?

I seed a ant hill. They runned everywhere. Like in the zoo.

Mommy dead like Daddy in the accident? Some kids don't have daddies because divorced. Divorced means mommies and daddies don't like each other. They disagreed. Sometimes Mommy and I disagree. We can't divorce. I'm good. All parts. People who are bad don't have families. We're okay. I don't remember my Daddy. Jamie's daddy didn't like his Mom any more. He went someplace far. Africa. New Jersey maybe. He hardly seed Jamie.

I lost? How I get back? I hate sleeping on ground. I cried. Maybe I never find anybody anymore. Where the road? Where Mrs. B.'s house? Road other way from stream. You cross one way, have to cross back. Right? Maybe I find somebody they like children. I was glad it was summer, not winter. I like snow though. Maybe I drink from the stream? It polluted? I drinked some. Only a little bit. I got more mud on my shirt. I wished I could go home. Maybe take a bath with my shark. I wished I had apple juice. I couldn't hide in crawl space . The Man knowed it. Lucky no rain. If Mommy here, she say, "Lovely day for the race Snoogums." Then I say, "What race?" I know the answer. I pretend I don't. Then Mommy says, "The human race." I laugh even though I know the joke. Mosquitoes bited me. I wished I could find a policeman or fireman or somebody else. Mommy say you lost, tell name and address. Dilly Thorne. Pepper Ridge Road. South Springport. Maine. United States. World. Solar system. Universe. I don't remember the zip code.

Which way town? I start now I get there before night time? How much miles?

"Mommy, come here!" I yelled. Could Man hear? I listened. Birds. Also a cricket. I sitted on a rock. I squished a bug by accident. He died. I don't like squishing. Mommy says stay away from water. Fountains okay. Stay away from ice in winter. Ice breaks. I wished I had something to eat. I wished I could hug Mommy. I wished I could pee. I peed.

The Man bad. He teasing when he said what his father did? It was pretty violent actually.

I heared a dog. Not Sir. Sir dead. It was the blond dog. Maybe I'd adopt him. He could make me company. Mommy wouldn't mind. How I feed him? I don't have any food. I tried whistling like Mommy. No whistle. The dog comed. He didn't wag. He barked and snapped. I got afraid. I seed his teeth. They were huge. He bited my shorts. I yelled, "Go away!" He didn't listen. He bited my knee. I tried to hit him. He ripped my shirt. I heared crashing.

Was Man coming? It was a big deer. It runned away. The dog runned after it. The dog taked a piece of my shirt.

I cried a lot. Probably three or four hours. My shirt torn. Mommy be mad? I could see blood on my knee and my hands. I put my hands in the stream.

I was careful. I washed the blood. All the time I cried. I walked some more. I listened. No dog. No Man. I had two enemies now. I comed to a place I could jump over the stream. I'm a good jumper. I fell in but I got out. I walked some more. Water swished in my boots. I comed to a big pile of leaves. I covered myself all over. I taked a nap.

SKIP

Mr. Bernstein took me in after it happened. He didn't officially adopt me because then he'd have to divide his money between me and his own kids, but he and Mrs. Bernstein, she told me to call her Marylou, were nice to me. They gave me the same things they gave their own kids except they didn't send me to the private schools their kids went to. I went to public school and the community college. One of their habits which annoyed me was that they were always talking about hard work and determination and getting ahead. Their favorite topic at dinner was stories about people who made it big in spite of enormous obstacles. They didn't mention that Mr. Bernstein got his money from his father who made a pile manufacturing ladies' clothes. But I have to admit they gave me a good start.

The first time I did it was when I was seventeen. High school kids were encouraged to do volunteer work once a week and

I picked the local shelter. This shelter was a building made over from something else and it had separate bedrooms for families. One little guy, who was about four years old, lived with his mother. She was a druggie and a prostitute. She was supposed to be getting treatment to kick the habit. She never paid any attention to her kid. The kid, William, was so grateful for a little attention it was pitiful. It was interesting to be mean to him one minute and act like his best friend the next. If I was nice he'd put his arms around my neck and kiss me over and over. When I was mean, he'd cry and hang on to my legs. He was really stupid. He followed me everywhere. He had no father. In that respect he was lucky. He had about eight brothers and sisters who were scattered in different foster homes.

The way it happened that first time was, I had a bunch of them in the playground. It started to get cold and all the kids were fighting and crying, so this other high school guy and I rounded them up and headed back. We got them inside and in the confusion of depositing them, nobody noticed when I took William with me when I left.

Did I plan it? Was it something I thought about all my life? I don't know.

The boss and his family were out skiing in Utah that week. They couldn't take me that time because I had a different school vacation from their own kids. So I had the house to myself.

Little William couldn't have been happier when I said I would take him to my house for the night.

He wasn't happy long. I kept him alive for two whole days and nights and he screamed the whole time.

I got the body out of the house before the family came home from Utah. I threw it in one of the local ponds. Some kids found it the next summer. They blamed one of the inmates of the shelter, an old wino didn't know his ass from his prick. He's probably still in prison. No one suspected me. I cried a lot.

That first time was different from the others. The mother didn't get to watch. The fly on the chest was a nice touch, I thought.

Father's body was never found.

TWENTY-THREE

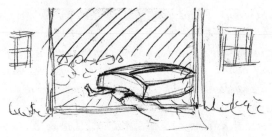

Sunday, June 10
Faith

Someone said, "Do you hear something?" and handed me a leaflet featuring an angelic looking child coupled incongruously with a weird thug. A small heart pulsed erratically. The screams, the unbearable swelling shrieks, beginning with terror and soaring into agony. I was in a train station where the departure board had no South Springport and the trains hurtled past, never stopping to pick up passengers. The retired man on the park bench said, "Son of a bitch sold off the subsidiaries and the rest of us got the shaft." "Jeff! Jeff!" the woman with Alzheimer's kept shouting, and Edith moved away a long time ago. A short man whose growth had been mysteriously stunted, asked, "You sure you once lived here?" and the land in back of the house sloped down to the familiar woods and the familiar stream and ascended to the familiar pine forest. I was lying on the floor of the swaying train, my head bumping against the seat, wondering where the conductors had gone.

Camping out was my idea. It was his third birthday and he invited his best friend, Teddy. Sand castles that didn't belong in the well kept garden; the outline of a child's body on the burlap bag; a house where there was no other sign of a child. Becky Schnell was nervous, regretting her decision to get into the tax assessor's office. A crackling of leaves, a break in the rhythm of the night and someone said, "Do you hear something?" "It's just a small animal, sweetie, a raccoon probably. Go back to sleep." The hulking blackness shut out the sky at the opening of the tent. And then it started. The screaming, the cataclysmic screaming.

A mad man was splicing the film and the story had no logical sequence. Drills pulsed in my head, shaking bits and pieces of memory loose. In the corridors of my mind I could hear the approaching steps of the torturers, the thundering boots of the conquering armies, the maddened roar of the lynch mob.

I sat up in bed. It was still dark outdoors. Whatever the doctor had injected into my veins was becoming diluted. Nausea and dizziness engulfed me.

It had happened a long time ago. The poor little body was dust by now. It had been at peace for years. Then why did the pain still gnaw at my vital organs? Why was I deafened by internal sirens warning me to hurry? The time for hurrying was long since past.

What could I have done differently? I had thought South Springport was a safe part of the world, far removed from the city's derelicts and murderers and rapists. How was I to know? Perhaps if I hadn't felt so safe. So sure that a noise outside the tent must be a cute little raccoon. Perhaps if I hadn't been so slow witted. Perhaps if I had had quicker reflexes. Perhaps if I had been trained in combat. Perhaps if I hadn't decided to camp out that night. Perhaps, perhaps, perhaps.

A lone woman with two small children in a wooded, secluded area in the middle of the night, and suddenly, from out of the slime, a festering, grotesque monster had appeared. A dark, faceless thing wrapping its talons around me, binding me in wire, but leaving my ears and my eyes free. If only I had been rendered blind and deaf. If only I had died instead of blocking out the memory and wandering the streets for years.

A thousand years wouldn't suffice to muffle those sounds drilled into my brain, to erase those sights that were driven into my eyes with burning needles. Unable to free myself, thrashing and pleading, I had listened to that Thing, that Corruption whispering, "Keep watching, Mother. You always liked to watch, Mother."

Bobby, oh my little Bobby. My darling baby with his large, trusting eyes, his infectious giggle, his warm cuddling body, his endless questing for knowledge, his convoluted turns of phrase. Bobby, who thought his mother could do anything. Begging Mommy to help him.

Then the silence. The awful final silence. The blessed silence. The nothingness. Deaf and blind at last. A nothingness where my precious little darling could float in peace. Where he would never be hurt or frightened again.

The excruciating smash to the head. The large duffle bag in which I was to make the journey to Boston. The evil, caressing whisper, "Have a nice trip, Mother. Live with it. Remember it always." Long tunnels of darkness, echoing cavernous spaces, a gently rocking journey to nowhere.

I was soaked with sweat. In the grey light I could just make out the four posters of the bed, the ghostly coverlet, the old fashioned chest and the rug on the floor. For the first time in many years, the usual questions about where was I, and who was I, didn't crowd around me. I was Faith Unger and I was in South Springport. And this was the Twenty-first Century.

I got out of bed. I was fully dressed. Someone had brought me back to Guy North's house and tucked me in after the doctor had given me the injection. I went to the kitchen and looked at the clock. A quarter to five. My head cluttered with sand castles, burlap bags, a deserted house, I looked out at the clear, starlit sky and the deserted ribbon of roadway. Terrified eyes were pleading, helpless hands were clutching. If I didn't hurry the unspeakable would happen. Again.

I went out through the mud room, across the small side porch with its stack of logs and headed for the garage. I would take Guy North's car. Then I hesitated. Would the keys be in the car? In the kitchen? In his room?

No car. To hell with it. If he heard me, he would prevent my going. Tell me I was mad. I would walk. I had spent years walking through leafy parks, along busy city streets, on empty subway platforms, past crowded docks. Searching for the irreplaceable.

There were no street lamps, but star and moonlight provided all the illumination I needed. Unhesitatingly, I made the two right turns, first onto Route 120 and then onto Pepper Ridge. I had to hurry. No more the helpless housewife, the bystander, the witness, the onlooker. This time I would stop it.

A car zipped by but I doubted the driver saw me. What would he or she have done if I'd been seen? The mad woman who had been bashed on the head, had lost her memory and something else infinitely more precious. Might she be intent upon a psychotic mission? Might they call the police? They too would have tried to thwart me. Luckily the insomniac Conrad Van Kuhn wasn't about.

The driveway just after the Buitenkamp house circled up about a thousand feet. The Jeep Wagoneer was still parked in front. I went up the flight of stairs and peered into the glass panel beside the front door. The moon shining in through the huge rear windows showed me a hall table with a vase of wilted tulips, a mirror, and beyond, part of a living room sofa.

On the left was a hallway and on the right two partially closed doors.

What would I say to the owners were I caught trespassing? "Pardon me. Do you happen to have a child who builds sand castles in a neighbor's neat garden and who sleeps on a burlap bag in a neighbor's garage?" But I didn't think I would be challenged. There was a brooding, forsaken air about the house.

Gently, I turned the knob. The door was locked. Back down the stairs to the rear where I saw a slide, a jungle gym, a swing and further into the woods, a tree house. And then, an oddity: someone had parked a car right on the lawn in back as if to conceal it.

The rear of the house was mostly glass, all of it uncurtained. In what was most certainly the master bedroom I saw a rumpled bed with no one in it. Beyond was a study with book lined shelves, a desk, chair, computer, telephone, fax machine. Next came a child's room with a crib, but the latter was so situated I couldn't see into it.

I tried the knob of a French door that led into the master bedroom, and this time it opened. Walk into my parlor . . . .

I walked back to the child's room. No child, but a Lilliputian table and two chairs, toy chest and vehicles, stuffed animals, papers and crayons, paints, clay, boat models, miniature garages, airports and supermarkets. Not a neat child. On the floor, a large plastic mat depicting a post office, school, park, homes, neat gray road. A town where nothing bad ever happened.

Back in the hallway, I went to one of the half closed doors I had seen from the front. As soon as I stepped across the threshold, I slipped and fell. A sliver of something sharp stung my thigh. The floor was covered with a sticky substance. It was still early dawn outside. Gingerly, I got to my feet and felt along the wall next to the entrance. I switched on the light.

Chaos. Pompeii after the lava arrived. The Mary Therese floating rudderless and people-less on a calm sea. A colonial settlement after the Indians attacked. Ordinary lives engulfed by instant disaster.

The kitchen floor was puddled by what I took to be juice. The counters were littered with food wrappers, banana peels, apples cores, body parts of a chicken. Interspersed with the edibles were toy tractors and trucks, a toy monkey, a pail and shovel showing the evidence of fresh dirt. A stool had been pulled to the sink.

I went through the house, switching on lights. A bathroom with evidence of a messy bath taker. A wet diaper in a pail. Beyond that, two neat, spotless rooms with flowered comforters, empty chests of drawers, empty closets. The master bedroom with the unmade bed had a closet filled with women's dresses, suits, slacks, blouses, and shoes. A bureau with neatly folded underwear, purses, gloves, scarves. No sign of a man. The exact opposite of Guy North's house. A woman living alone with a child. Where was the woman? Lying on the floor of an Amtrak train bound for nowhere? Where was the child? A broken thing abandoned in the woods?

I went down to the basement. A game room with a ping pong table, sofas, stacks of game. Against one wall were two sets of skis, one for an adult and one for a small child, boots, skates, large and small bicycles. On the other side of the stairs was a dusty, unused looking workroom with an electric saw and tools hanging on a bulletin board. A large hole cut out in the cement wall led to what appeared to be a crawl space. Peering in, I found the light switch and pressed it. Inside was the usual clutter of boxes, trunks, ancient furniture.

Noticing something out of the way, I climbed up onto the work table, and squatting down, crabbed my way into the crawl space. What had caught my attention was that, although most of the boxes and furniture were neatly stacked, a doll house had been dismantled, odd bits of furniture and the dolls scattered. Smashed Christmas ornaments glittered on the cement floor. I was still trying to assess the significance of these facts when I noticed a disturbance in a far corner. A trunk had been pulled away from the wall, and behind it, was a child's worn out comforter and the remains of a picnic.

What was the house trying to tell me? A disordered bedroom, an incredibly messy kitchen, neat guest rooms and living room, a hiding place for a child in a crawl space, a car hidden next to the woods. People didn't leave their homes in this condition when going on vacation. The whole place was one huge question mark, and my mind was a switchboard of flashing messages, but the confusion inside my head overrode the exact wording of the dispatch.

Upstairs again, I looked out of the large rear window. In the gradual pearling of the sky, I could see the outlines of a pool, a paddock and a barn. I went out, searching for something I didn't want to see ever again.

When I caught sight of the object floating in the pool, my first instinct was to run. Instead I raised my eyes to heaven and said, "Please God, no, please God." And then, in the grizzled light I could see the fur of a dark haired animal. A dog. "Thank you, God," I whispered.

Nonetheless, I was nearly overpowered by apprehension. This upper middle class house with its rolling lawns and its pool and its paddock seemed like a candy coating over a rotting interior. Like a Uriah Keep of inanimate objects, it was overly sweet on the surface, but underneath it reeked of –

Hurry.

I passed a rock garden and crossed a paddock with homemade tire jumps (but no horse) and approached the barn. For a moment I stopped in the dusky light to listen but all I heard was a sweet chorus of early morning bird song. I slid back the heavy doors of the barn and fumbled for a light switch but couldn't locate one. Cautiously I went in and nearly stumbled against a bulky object on the concrete floor. A small sailboat. Gradually, other objects came into focus. Rough stalls, a smattering of hay, two rubberized buckets.

I almost tripped again. Catching hold of the boat, I looked down at the new obstruction and couldn't believe what I was seeing. A human foot sticking out from under the boat.

Only in New York City was one supposed to find bodies littering benches, storefronts, hot air grates. Not in suburban barns.

A woman's foot, bare. I watched it in horror, half expecting it to start walking on its own. Blackness threatened to overcome me. I had a notion that if I ran back to the house to call the police, the foot would no longer be there when I returned. Then everyone would know for sure that I was mad. I picked up a corner of a horse blanket that lay on the ground near the foot, too terrified to lift it up entirely, and came upon a second foot. Not a mate to the first but of an entirely different variety. It was wearing black flats and green slacks.

I began to sway.

It was a charnel house. Dead dog. Two dead women. Time to get help.

If the bodies were still here when the police arrived, everyone would finally have to pay attention. I would no longer be a homeless derelict with hallucinations of horror. I would be a homeless derelict with plenty of proof.

I was running back to the house when the screaming started.

TWENTY-FOUR

Sunday, June 10
Dilly

I wished I had a egg. I wished I could go to the Red Dragon with Mommy like the olden days. Duck and extra dumplings. Also a fortune cookie. I like fortune cookies. Not the taste. One fortune said I had determination. Determination is never give up. Also success. What's success? I kicked rocks. Mommy said look up when you walk. I looked up. Beautiful sky Mommy says. The sky is dark. Is that beautiful? I tried to remember before when I had a Mommy. I wished I had pancakes. I was pretty bored. I play alone when Mommy does chores, but only a little bit. Mostly somebody entertains me. I'm a help in the supermarket. Once I finded the pancake box and putted it in the cart. Mommy said, "You reading these days, Dill Pickle?" Mommy taked me to the office when Cindy can't babysit me. She never leaved me alone before. In the office she gived me pencils and paper. I writed letters. Saturdays we goed to the playground. Sometimes the woods. Once to a play, Pinocchio. About a boy who lied. His nose growed. In winter we slided. Also I have skates. Once I skied between Mommy's knees. Sometimes I have a play date with Chris or Tracy. Moore taked us to the circus. I hated it.

Especially when the man shooted out of the cannon. The zoo's okay. Also the aquarium and the restoration. Also the Carbeen. Is this my whole life? Other part gone? Is this dead? I wish I *was* dead with Mommy making me company. Cindy said dead is heaven. This heaven? You can't see heaven. Who takes care of me in heaven? Mommy? The guys who live with God? Angels? Angels are like the tooth fairy. They're polite.

They say please and thank you and you're welcome.

Which way home? I could lie next to Mommy. No, Man might come. Mommy said never go with strangers. Man a stranger? A bird made noises because I was bothering it. Maybe it had babies. I wished I could see the bird babies. "You like worms?" I said. "Want me find you a worm?" It flied away.

I eated grass. It had no taste. A airplane in the sky. Was people there? They see me? I waved. Maybe they waved back. I can't tell. The stewardess asks do you want soda. Never push emergency button. Never. Lightning can't hurt. Maybe. I hate thunder. Never touch matches. Never. Ever. They can burn you.

I walked home. Maybe ten miles. Maybe not. I wished I had Curious George. Or a banana. Or cappuccino like in the museum before Mommy dead. I jumped up and down. I sitted and taked off my boots and shaked out the dirt. I heared dogs. I was afraid. Some dogs nice. Make me company. That yellow dog bad. Really mean. I hate that dog. I hate sleeping on leaves. The ants bite.

I comed to my own tree house. How? I don't know. I looked through the trees. No Man. Moore said it's my own secret hiding place. I climbed. I taked off my boots. It was pretty comfortable. I heared noise. Somebody coming. Man standing on the ladder. I couldn't run. Man in the way.

"I don't like this," I said. "This is no fun. I hate it. I'm thirsty."

"Soon you won't be thirsty."

'You give me a soda?"

"Soda bad for your teeth."

"I want my Mommy."

"Soon you be with her."

"When?"

He told me I was bad because I runned away. He said "You know what Father did to me when I was bad?" I putted my hands on my ears.

"I don't like that," I said. "I want my Mommy."

He said, "Your mommy went away like my mommy."

I said, "Why your mommy went away?"

"She hate me," he said. I said I didn't believe him.

He sitted next to me and he hurted me. I said, "I don't like that."

He said, "Stop that crying. I hate sissies."

I said, "I want Curious George."

He said, "You played a trick on me. You made the mirror laugh."

"That was the light," I said.

He hurted me bad. I wasn't brave.

SKIP

Why?

That's the question the police always ask serial killers when they catch them. Why?

What was he like?

That's the question the police always ask the neighbors.

He was a nice guy, they say. Responsible, helpful. Quiet. Kept to himself. Ever hear of a chatty serial killer? Kinda' guy who'd buy you a beer? Almost never. You'd think they'd put anklets on real quiet people. Keep an eye on them.

Sometimes when I wake up I don't know who I am or where I am. I seem to be changing places with somebody else.

Can I stop? If I stop now they'll never catch me. It'll be another unsolved crime. Can I stop?'

I keep remembering Father's face when he did what he did to me. It wasn't only anger. It was something else.

That's why.

It's enjoyable.

TWENTY-FIVE

Sunday, June 10
Faith

The screaming on a night in June seventeen years ago and the screaming on a morning in June seventeen years later coalesced into a single deranged nightmare. The years evaporated and I was back in a tent at the campground and a childish voice was querying, "Do you hear something?" I was drowning in terror and the sounds I heard now were a hideous echo of my worst agony, the cause of my long self-induced trance.

Why hadn't I torn off my hands in a greater effort to free them? Why had I allowed my baby to die that way? Why hadn't I reacted sooner, grabbed the two of them and escaped when the tiny voice had asked, "Do you hear something?"

But God was doing what He rarely did. He was giving me a second chance. This time I'd had seventeen years to prepare.

This time I would save my little darling and rejuggle the puzzle pieces of Gaza. Or else die. Slip into that peace. This time I'd escape for good.

The high-pitched screaming, the screaming of a child in fear or worse, came from beyond the pool, beyond the barn, beyond the paddock. But from where? I was in a state of befuddlement and I bolted back and forth uselessly. A weapon. I needed a weapon but I couldn't waste time running to the house for a poker or a knife. I whirled dementedly, searching the barn. Rubberized buckets, horseshoes, bags of cement, chicken wire in rolls, fence posts, ladder, chlorine drums, paint cans.

Horseshoe? No. I would have to get too close and he could overpower me. If I threw it, I would probably miss.

Fence post?

One was broken and I grabbed a three-foot segment and began running in the direction of the screaming. Gears, meshing inside my head, began working me out of my swaddled state, propelling me across the lawn, under the paddock fence and into the woods. As if I'd been training seventeen years for this Olympian moment, I thrashed through the mulched leaves, the high grasses and the fallen branches while the screaming rose to a crescendo.

The bedlam pierced my skull, lacerated my chest, but I muffled my sobs so that I could catch the monster off guard. In my endless nightmare he had grown to an impossible size, achieved gargantuan strength. I needed every advantage I could muster. Obviously, he was convinced there was no one within hearing distance. I tripped over a downed tree trunk, ripped the palms of my hand on some brambles, caught my hair on a branch, running towards that God-awful noise and finally I reached a clearing where I gyrated in confusion. Where was the screaming coming from? God, help me. Please, God, let me get there in time. Don't let it happen again.

Behind me came a low humming, as of the first warning of a disturbance of nature. Before I could identify the sound, a brown and black tornado leapt upon my back. If I hadn't been so taut, so primed for mayhem, I might have lost my weapon and gone down under the huge, furry body and mouthful of fangs. But as it was, I spun around without even seeing what it was, and smashed at the creature with my broken fence post. The animal toppled back into the grass and then started scrambling away, almost on all fours into the bushes. I swung the fence post and threw it but it fell harmlessly to the ground, well behind the thing.

It would be back and all chance of surprise was gone. Would I have to watch helplessly once again? Was it all going to repeat itself?

But instinct beyond reason provided me with an alternative. Filled with hatred, wanting to strike out, crush, demolish, maim, mutilate, instead I began to screech, "Come here! Over here! I've got the bastard!" I careened in another direction, and shouted into the woods. "Circle! Don't let him get away!" Deepening my voice I squalled, "Spread out! Get the son of a bitch!" A dog howled, the child screamed, I ducked down, picked up rocks and threw them in the direction of where the monster had crawled away into the dark shadows.

Does a freak of nature pause to think when he's on the verge of an unimaginable crime? Does a creature beyond humanity take time to unravel the likely from the unlikely? Does a rabid wolf being run to ground think clearly?

Evidently not.

Amid the clamor of the dog, the shrieks of the child and my own bellowing, I heard the sound of feet plunging through the underbrush, heading away from me towards the car parked on the lawn. Then the roar of a motor disappearing down the driveway.

I continued twirling like a mechanized top unable to wind down. The pandemonium diminished to whining on the part of the dog, whimpering on the part of the child. Where was the latter? Hovering in the sky?

Finally, in the grey dawn light, I spotted it above my head. A rough structure of boards about twelve feet from the ground, built in the crotch of a huge maple tree.

I climbed up the primitive ladder – pieces of wood nailed into the tree – and came to a platform.

On a patch of an ancient oriental rug, amid scattered leaves and pine needles, its clothing torn, its skin bloodied, something pale lay curled up, sobbing.

The object of my quest. The end of the trail.

Gently, I turned the demented little thing over so that I could lift it in my arms. I held it to my breast. It clung to me. Suddenly he reared back his head.

"You're not my Mommy!" he bawled.

I screamed. "You're not Bobby!"

I dropped it back onto the rug.

TWENTY-SIX

Saturday, June 23
Dilly

Mommy say all the time, "Tell me more." I say, "What that you writing?" She say, "Shopping list." I try take it away. She won't let me. I was frustrated of her. Every time I talk she writes.

I don't mind staying in the hospital with Mommy. Moore bringed my toys. The nurse said, "This room like F.A.O. Schwarz." I know that place. Geoff and Peg taked me once. Geoff and Peg my grandfather, grandmother. The hospital like my room at home. Full of my stuff. I get bored of museums and playgrounds. I like playing in my room. It's peaceful.

Susie is almost all better. Mommy soon better. Susie said I can't stay in the hospital all the time with Mommy. She take me to her house. I don't mind. Except Chris grabs a lot. Susie makes me walk on streets a lot. In stores. Library even. Church. I say, "Why we walk all the time?" She say, "You recognize anybody?" I recognize lots. She bothers me.

Moore says hospital room like a Marx Brothers skit. "What Mark Brothers skit?" I said. He said it's when people crowd in tiny place. Mrs. B. says it smells like flower shop. She hugs a lot. She says she sorry she not home. She couldn't help it. The flowers make a nice smell. Geoff gave me a farm machinery catalogue to pick a tractor. "How 'spensive this?" I said to Mommy. She said, "Too 'spensive for you." Her head is bandaged except for hair sticking out one side. She look like a mummy at the museum. Mommy mummy. She kisses me all the time. I don't mind. The bed is filled with Curious George and me and the moose, rabbit, a front-end loader, a bulldozer, a box of pencils and a pad and maybe a hundred books. Ten even. I zoomed the front end loader and the nurse said, "Don't hurt Mommy." Mommy hugged some more. She said, "Hurt me all you want." Faith, the lady who saved me from the Man, says nothing practically. She leans against the wall. Policemen come all the time, ask Mommy questions. She tells. They say, "Tell again."

She says, "I heared something in the hall. Like somebody tripping over a toy maybe."

"Where the dog?" policeman ask. He meaned Sir.

"No barking," Mommy said. "I think he already dead."

"Then what?" the policeman ask. No uniform. Mommy says he wears plain clothes. They're not so plain. Maybe plaid. Very nice.

Mommy said, "I don't know. Was unconscious." Unconscious is you know something but you don't know you know it. Mommy said, "Why didn't I call police first? Not go in myself."

Faith said, "He hit harder than he meaned. He likes mothers watch."

"Watch what?" I said.

Policeman ask more questions. Even more than me. Ask me questions too. I said I forgot. I said he hurted a lot. Also told me story about wasp and fly. Policeman ask what color Man's eyes. I forgot. He big? I don't know.

Policeman say, "Why he keep leaving? Not finish his business?"

I say, "What business?"

Policeman ask Faith what he look like.

She say, "I scared him away with noise."

Policeman say, "What he look like long ago?"

She say, "It was dark."

Mommy say, "What about other mothers?"

Policeman say, "They moved away. We find them soon."

Faith say, "How many?"

Policeman say, "Maybe four. Or five. Far as we know. We're still checking with other police departments."

I say, "Five what?" Nobody told me.

Policeman say to Faith, "Tell me again."

Faith say, "I was camping with Bobby and Teddy."

"Who Bobby and Teddy?" I said. Nobody told me.

Faith told policeman, "Bobby said, 'You hear a noise?' "

I said, "What noise?" Nobody told me.

Faith said, "He tie me with wire. I wish I died."

Mommy said, "Thank God you not died."

Policeman ask a hundred questions more. "What about Teddy?"

"He runned away when Man tying me," Faith said.

Mommy said, "Somebody take Dilly in hall."

I yelled and kicked. I said, "It's okay. I don't know what you're talking about anyway." They letted me stay.

Policeman said, "Why Bobby not run?"

Faith said, "He feeled safe with his mommy."

"Why Faith crying?" I said. Nobody told me. I was frustrating of this.

Faith said, "Bobby begged."

I said, "For money? Like homeless people?" I was sorry for her. She was nice. She chased the Man.

Faith said, "He hitted me on head when all over."

"What over?" I said.

"I waked up on train," Faith said.

"Why train?" Policeman asked.

Faith didn't know. I didn't either.

"Why he not kill mothers?" policeman said.

"He wants them watch and remember," Faith said.

I didn't ask what remember.

Everybody talked a lot. I got bored of it. Nobody entertaining me.

Policeman ask where Mommy's husband. Mommy said he dead. Faith's husband divorced. Policeman said Man come only to places where no husbands.

Geoff said, "How he know where no husbands?"

Peg said, "He works in small towns."

Susie comed with Chris. I telled Chris, Geoff buying me a new tractor.

"Share?" Chris said. I said I give him my Massey Ferguson. It's broken anyway.

Policeman ask Susie more questions. Man smell of smoke? He big? She hear him breathe? Susie didn't know.

Mommy said, "You think he come back?"

"I don't want him back!" I yelled.

Peg telled me she and Geoff stay at house until Mommy home. Also Moore. Also a policeman.

Moore comed. He said, "Hi, Pardner." I telled him Geoff buying me a tractor. He said, "Share?" He fooling me.

Faith said, "He looked like Dilly."

I said, "Who?"

Faith telled me. "Bobby. Blue eyes. Blond hair."

"Where Bobby is?"

Nobody telled me.

Policeman said, "All the kids like that."

Susie said, "Brown hair, brown eyes safe?"

Mommy said, "Chris safe anyway. You have husband."

Mrs. B. said, "The killer in Atlanta only killed little black boys. Killer black. So this killer blue eyed, blond?"

Peg said, "He kill mostly around here. Somebody must know him. How come nobody suspect?"

Mommy said, "Nobody suspect Bundy."

I said, "Who Bundy?" Nobody told me.

Moore bringed Mommy grapes. I said to Chris, "You want a grape? They're fresh."

Mrs. B. said, "Bundy looked like a lawyer."

Susie say to me, "Why you not ask what lawyer is?" She fooling me. I know what lawyer is. Mommy a lawyer.

Susie said, "What turns people into monsters?"

Chris said, "People turn to monsters?" He didn't know she teasing.

Moore said, "Everybody looking for answer."

I climbed on bed and kissed Mommy. I said, "How your day?" I heared a sound and I grabbed Mommy and I yelled.

Mommy said, "Why you yelling?"

I told her in her ear. "Man make that sound."

"What sound?"

"I don't know."

Everybody whispering. What they whispering?

Moore said, "Hey , Pardner, how about you and me go out for a huge ice cream cone? Ben and Jerry's?"

I said, "Bring it here."

Chris said, "Me too?"

Mommy said, "What scared you, Snoogums?"

I didn't know. Really didn't. Not pretend.

People comed in. People goed out. More whispering. Geoff said, "Come on, Dill. We can also pick up the new tractor."

"You bring it here." I hugged Mommy some more.

"We'll all go," Geoff said. "Susie and Chris, Faith, Peg and Moore."

"I wanna' stay with Mommy."

"I need to nap, Dill Pickle," Mommy said.

Policeman said, "You don't come, you don't get tractor."

"Really?" I said.

"Come on, Dillon," Moore said.

"How big the tractor?"

Geoff said, "Big enough you can ride it."

"When I get it?"

"Right after we do one thing."

"I don't like that."

"Let's go, Dill," Geoff said.

"The Man be there?" I said.

Everybody stop talking. Mrs. B. laugh. Geoff taked my hand. "What make you think that?" he said.

"The sound," I said.

"Come on," Moore said. "First one stop. Then ice cream. Then the tractor."

"It's bribery," Mommy said.

"What's bribery?"

"You acting like a pill, Dilly," Mommy said.

"First tractor," I said.

"Right after," Geoff said.

"Man very strong," I said.

"Not as strong as all of us," Moore said.

I kissed Mommy. I jumped off the bed. I'm a good jumper. I taked Moore's hand. Also Geoff's.

I said, "First the tractor."

"Right afterwards," Geoff said.

Faith said, "I want to come."

Policeman said, "I counting on it."

"Why counting on it?" I said.

Nobody telled me.

SKIP

I'm pretty sure nobody suspects me. Why should they? I'm an ordinary hard working member of the community. I'm friendly, but I never get too chummy. If I keep my distance, I can't make mistakes. I never do it in my own house because they can trace nearly everything these days.

I wish I didn't get confused some times. I can't always remember which event I dreamed and which actually happened. And those blackouts are getting more frequent. I pray they never happen in front of people. Grownups anyway.

Why should this prayer be answered when the others never were?

The newspapers are full of it. And not just locally. **FLY KILLER STRIKES AGAIN.** *Maybe I shouldn't have gotten fancy with those flies. It's the kind of gimmick everyone loves. Probably why I picked it in the first place. These murders would attract attention in any case.*

How I hated Mother. How I still hate her wherever she may be. More than I hated Father. Her favorite expression: "Wait'll I tell your father." Then she always watched with that expression on her face.

That's why I don't kill the mothers. I want them to watch and then spend the rest of their lives hearing the way their kids screamed and begged and promised to be good.

I always promised to be good. For all the good it did me. I'd grab her around the knees and beg her not to tell. She always did..

I didn't plan the first one, little William who lived in the shelter with his mother. It just happened. In his case, his mother never got to watch. She probably wouldn't have cared anyway, she was so drugged out. They pinned that one on the old wino. Who would suspect a volunteer from the high school?

Nobody ever suspected what Father did either. Well, maybe that black social worker. She didn't swallow Father's lies when she found me in the closet. But she never did anything. Maybe she couldn't. Her superiors probably told her to forget it. It was unprovable.

Once the boss' wife caught sight of my back. She let out a yelp and began grilling me. I told her I'd had a bad accident on my bike once and I think she believed me. Or pretended to. Why didn't I ever tell anybody the truth after Father died? Because then they might have gotten suspicious about the boating accident. I used the boating accident as an excuse to never go swimming. I couldn't take a chance on anyone seeing me in swimming trunks. That was the reason I never got married. No it wasn't. The reason I never got married was women didn't interest me. Only little boys.

I can still see Father's eyes when he was trying to hang onto the boat and I smashed and smashed at his knuckles. God, that felt good. Turning the tables on him. The boss never heard him. Not with the radio and the wind and the boss being in the head. He took all the blame himself. His conscience bothered him for years. Was that the reason he took me in?

Why didn't that nice nurse in the hospital do anything? She was the best person I ever knew but she also let Father talk her out of it. I fell down a flight of stairs, I think he told her. Jesus, people are stupid. Or they don't care enough.

If people hadn't been stupid or had cared more, none of it would have happened.

My memory of the other kids has grown hazy, but I'll never forget little William. Nobody had ever paid any attention to him before. He was so grateful. He never held a grudge. If I was mean he'd forget it the next minute. If I was kind, he'd hang on like a barnacle. Talking about barnacles, we sailed a lot, the boss, his family and me. He said I had to keep doing it so I could recover from the memory. God, people are stupid.

I'll get that little Dilly yet. The little shit. Fooling me with the mirror and then dashing off into the woods. Then, when I finally had him, the damned posse arrived. How did they find out? Who warned them?

The mothers always blame themselves. They keep thinking, why did I ever turn my back on him in that crowded store? Or, why did I forget to lock the doors that night? Or, why did I leave him alone for a few minutes while I did my errands? Or, why did I ever go camping that night?

What they don't know is that nothing would have helped. Once I focus on a kid, I do my homework. I pick a woman without a man in the house. I learn her routine. If it doesn't work out one way, it will work out another. I'm patient. I can wait. They don't have a chance. I've never fucked up. Except for Dilly.

Nobody knows what I look like because it's either dark or I wear a stocking over my head. Sometimes a ski mask.

Dilly's the first one to get away and the first one who can identify me. I have to keep out of his way, but still keep to my routine. That shouldn't be hard. Our paths don't have to cross.

It might be a good idea to move out of this area. How would I earn a living? Would it create suspicion if I leave?

I used to think about consulting a psychiatrist, but I decided against it. All that talk about confidentiality isn't worth a shit when it comes to the crunch.

I'll get Dilly and then I'll quit. Find a quiet place and keep him alive for days where nobody can hear him. He's even interesting to talk to. After him I'll quit. I can't push my luck forever. Maybe I can join T.A. Torturers Anonymous.

TWENTY-SEVEN

Saturday, June 23
Faith

"Can I ask her a question?" Dilly said to Moore Foster, either his uncle or a friend of his mother's. He pointed to a heavy black police woman who standing beside the front desk at the police station.

Uneasily, Moore said, "I guess so, Pardner."

Dilly pointed to the police woman's protruding stomach. "You got a baby in there?"

The woman laughed. "No, but you just started me on a diet."

"How babies come out?" was Dilly's next question. In order to look at the woman's face, he had lean back so far that he nearly sent his ice cream cone somersaulting over his head. His grandmother, the woman he called Peg, snatched the cone in time.

"Ask your mother," the police woman said, pointing mistakenly to Susie, his mother's friend.

Dilly was momentarily confused but his first priority was gathering information, not pointing out inaccuracies. "Girls can be policemen sometimes?"

"This kid needs a course in political correctness," the policewoman said.

Deciding he was pumping a dry well, Dilly refocused his attention.

"What Geoff up to?" he asked Peg. Geoff, his grandfather, was speaking softly to a group of men.

Vaguely, Peg said, "Oh, he's discussing a problem."

"Some problems you decide yourself. Not car accidents. You don't decide those."

I was next on his list. "How you get unmarried?"

"You go to a judge." I was torn between wanting to, and hating to, stare at his inquisitive beautiful little face.

"I have a Mommy still. Just my Daddy's dead."

I nodded faintly.

"You live outside on the street?"

"Yes."

"How you cook? You sleep on cardboard? You have a table?"

"People give me food."

"Who give you food?"

"People who work in shelters."

"What is shel – "

"Dilly," Peg said, "You sure ask a lot of questions."

"You're bothering my idea."

Back to me. "Why you live outside on the street?"

"I don't have a home."

"That because you're bad?"

While I was considering, he asked the policewoman, "You have a gun?"

"Yup."

"Can I see it?"

The policewoman looked around helplessly at her grinning co-workers. In addition to our own contingent – me, Dilly, Dilly's friend Chris, Chris' mother Susie, Moore, Geoff and Peg – the police station was crowded with people in uniform. and plain clothes. The policewoman took out her gun and held it up for Dilly's inspection,

"What kind is?"

"Glock nine millimeter."

"Can I hold it?"

Playtime was over. "No way."

Unfazed, he asked a detective, "How you be a policeman?"

"You go to policeman's school."

"I'm going to truck driver school. Was trucks when you a little boy?"

The detective looked baffled. "What?"

"He wants to know if motorized vehicles were invented when you were young," interpreted Moore.

Chris, who didn't share Dilly's hunger for knowledge, said, "Can we go home?"

"I send poor kids my broken toys," Dilly said. He was back talking to the overweight black policewoman.

"Why not send them toys that aren't broken?" She asked.

For once Dilly was speechless.

People eddied around us, some departing, newcomers arriving. Telephones kept buzzing. Car tires screeched outdoors. I was in the eye of the storm. I sat on a bench and examined a jade plant. Each leaf had its dark and light sides, depending upon where the sun hit. Passersby kept darting quick, curious glances in my direction and then averting their eyes. Even in my new clothes, I wore the stigma of a disaster survivor. A stigma that would never leave me.

And then, in the midst of the background cadences, Dilly screamed. He dropped his ice cream cone on the floor and literally climbed up Geoff to reach his encircling arms. He was shrieking.

"The Man! The Man!"

August Gunther, who had just entered the police station and was heading for the rear, stopped, transfixed. Finally he turned around. As his eyes lit on Dilly, his face lost all expression. Then, without hurrying, and as if he had just recalled a prior commitment, he reversed direction.

All the seemingly random activity in the crowded room suddenly coalesced. Those who had been lolling, apparently aimlessly, and those who had been wandering back and forth, apparently without purpose, united like bits in a kaleidoscope to form a design. Front and back doors were suddenly blocked. What had been a meandering stream was transformed into a dammed reservoir.

I stared at Augie Gunther's handsome features, at his ex-football star's athletic frame, at his pleasant All American appearance. I was back in the dark, a huge shape filling the folded back flap of the tent, and a little voice asking, "Do you hear something?"

"What's going on, Captain?" Augie asked, trying to be heard above Dilly's shrieking.

The slightly older, slightly heavier man he addressed as captain, walked around Geoff to peer at Dilly's partially buried face. "Dilly, you know this man?" Dilly dug his face in further and continued howling.

"Augie, you ever see this kid before?"

Augie glanced at the back of Dilly's head. His tanned, healthy skin seemed to have become slightly puckered, like an overripe apple. Finally, he shrugged. "Who can tell? I see kids all day long." Slowly he looked around. "Hi there Faith. What are you doing here?"

I couldn't unglue my eyes. Voices and images swarmed in my head like maddened bees. I wanted to run but I could no more move my body than my eyes. My brain threatened to explode and blow me into oblivion. From a blurry distance I heard the captain say, "Read him his rights" and Augie laughed. The laugh was like a sound erupting from a long buried coffin. Augie smiled at his fellow officers and a few smiled back uncertainly.

"Look up, Dilly," the captain said.

"No!" Dilly shouted.

"Come on, Pardner," Moore urged. "Nobody is going to hurt you."

Dilly ground his face into his grandfather's sport shirt.

"Dilly," the captain said gently, "You don't help us, some other kid might get hurt."

"A kid get hurt?" Dilly's muffled voice asked.

"It's possible, if you don't help us."

"The Man hurt me?"

"No way. We've got the whole South Springport police force here to protect you."

"He come when I sleep?"

"We won't let him."

"He know the crawl space. Also the tree house."

"Dilly, is this the man who hurt you?"

Clinging tightly to his grandfather's neck, Dilly peeked sideways. "I don't see him," he whispered.

"The other way."

Reluctantly, Dilly turned his head. August Gunther smiled but Dilly buried his face and whispered. "That's the Man."

"Louder, Dilly."

"That's the Man."

"You're sure?"

"He told me story about the fly and the wasp."

August Gunther said, "What's the kid talking about? I never saw him before in my life."

"You never saw him before?" the captain said.

"Well maybe around town. I can't tell one kid from another."

"We've had dozens of guys passing through here and you're the only one he identified."

"This is crazy. What made you bring him here anyway?"

"He heard one of our beepers going off in the hospital this morning and he said it was the same sound the man made the couple of times he had to leave Dilly."

"A beeper?" August Gunther laughed incredulously. "Everybody and his uncle can carry a beeper."

"For two weeks now we've walked Dilly up and down the streets of this town, through local stores, into public buildings and offices and he never identified anyone else."

"That's crap and you know it, Captain."

Joining the throng in my congested brain was the memory of Augie Gunther and me driving up towards Dilly's house. Nearly at the crest of the drive his beeper had gone off. We'd had to turn back before we could investigate further.

I cleared my throat. "Captain, can a person activate his own beeper?"

"Sure, if he practices a bit."

"That's what he did once when we were at the Thorn house." I explained the incident of the sand castles and the aborted drive up the Thorn's driveway. "He didn't want me to go into that house. We turned around in the driveway."

"Jesus," August Gunther said, "Faith is a victim of amnesia." He caught my eyes again and I couldn't demagnetize them. "She's completely confused. A homeless vagrant wandering the streets of Boston for seventeen years – "

"How do you know it was seventeen years?" the captain asked.

"It must have come up at some – "

"You know it's seventeen years because that's when you murdered her little boy?"

"If you're going to believe a hysterical kid and a mentally disturbed woman, I guess I'd better have a lawyer. And by the way, for the record, you still haven't read me my rights."

"He got afraid when he heard the laughing mirror Moore gave me," Dilly said. He was gaining confidence, expanding like a dried paper flower which, when placed in water, doubles in size.

"Laughing mirror?" asked the captain.

"Laughing mirror," Augie Gunther said with asperity. "Beepers. Did you ever hear such shit?"

"I teared his sleeve," Dilly continued, cockier with every passing minute. "I bited him. Like the dog bited me."

Augie Gunther held up both hands. "Boy bites man? Where was I bitten then?" The hands were smooth.

Moore said, "You've had time to heal."

Wasps buzzed in my head. They were joined by swarms of flies, bees, mosquitoes and locusts. Scenes slid by as if on a fast forward tape: a missing little girl coupled with a weird looking monster. A man on a bench saying, "There's no justice in the world." A small hand gripping mine as I skated around a pond. A train rocking in the night. A child strangled by a suspect arrested for a previous murder but released for lack of evidence. Wooded trails and a stream where I walked, a small prattling figure at my side. A voice lisping, "This is the church, this is the steeple, open the doors and see all the people." A headline shouting, "Body of missing three year old found." A small boy asking, "He come when I sleep?" A screaming in the night that would go on forever.

I looked at August Gunther. His face oscillated as if under water. One moment kindly and compassionate; the next, the quintessence of infinite evil. Everyone else was watching him too, their eyes flickering alternately with belief and disbelief, like clouds on a windy day.

How could one not believe him? A police lieutenant, square jawed, blue eyed, handsome. A former football player. Not a jury in the world would convict him.

I was jammed next to the overweight black policewoman. I could feel something hard on her hip, something that was within easy reach of my hand. Moving carefully, as if I were playing "pick up sticks", I slid her gun from its holster – she had failed to close it after showing it to Dilly – raised it and fired into August Gunther's face.

TWENTY-EIGHT

Sunday, June 24
Dilly

Faith shooted the Man. She taked the police lady's gun and shooted. Not two hands like TV. Man's face pff. I didn't mind. I wanted look some more. Peg holded me and didn't let me. I kicked. I holded my ears. Everybody yelled. Policeman putted handcuffs on Faith. I was sorry. They putted her in jail. I telled them she very nice actually. They didn't listen.

Peg buyed me the John Deere. I can drive it. I said I was sorry I kicked. Next day she kicked me. She said we even. She didn't hurt. She was wearing socks. She made me go to barber. I hated that. Those guys do a bad job.

Mommy said, "What happen to Faith now?"

Moore said probably get out on bail. Take couple days to process.

I said, "What bail is? What process is?"

Mommy said, "Bail is money so Faith not in jail."

"Forever?" I said.

"Has to be a trial."

"What trial is?"

"Jury says if Faith is guilty."

"What jury is?"

"Go to the dictionary." She fooling me.

"Who gives money?" I said.

"Guy North." He leaned his house, Mommy said. His house leaning? Will it fall down? No one telled me.

I telled Mommy get food delivered to hospital. Beer for her. Soda for me. Maybe hot tea. Pizza. No pepperoni.

"You bored of hospital food, Dill Pickle?" Mommy said.

Moore bringed a pizza. The room smelled nice. There were lots of flowers. Can flowers connect again and grow? I wished I could kill a rabbit. Look inside. It's interesting. Like the Man's face. Is rabbit delicious? Rabbit like to be eated?

I was pretty bored of the hospital. Actually I have lots of energy. I want a gun when I grow up. My other grandmother in Washington said she send me gun some day. That's a long time from now. For shooting targets. Not people. Not animals. I drawed a picture to send her. I telled Mommy what to write. If Man comed again I'll cut off his head. My grandmother doesn't live with the president. The other Washington. She too sick to come. Has 'thritis.

I have lots of money. Real and pretend. Also a credit card. I hope the Man never comes again. Not ever. Never.

Mommy has a friend is breast feeding. She closes one when the baby drinks from the other. I play gentle. Not rough like Chris and Tracy. My new raincoat has reflectors. People see me in the dark. Moore taked me to New York City to see the Intrepid long ago. I wasn't afraid in the submarine. I asked the guard questions. He didn't know. The carrier was okay.

I climbed on Mommy's bed. I said, "Mommy you be happy soon?" She said she never happier in life. I said, "Where Man Now?" She said, "Dead." I said, "Bones break when you die?" She said," Stop talking about dying." I said, "Why you always write when I talk?"

TWENTY-NINE

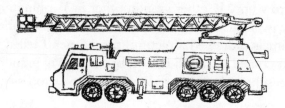

Sunday, July 24
Faith

"I don't know what made me stop growing. My mother and father looked normal."

Absently, I traced Guy's lips with my forefinger and moved closer so that our bodies contacted at more points. Since he'd shaved off the mustache and beard, his lips and chin had emerged as if rust had been scraped from a fine but neglected work of sculpture.

"You have a nice mouth," I told him.

"Nature balances its debits and credits." He pulled me even closer so that the contact points were more like fusions.

I stared over his head at a patch of gray-blue sky. "That accounts for Augie Gunther's handsome face and internal rot?"

"He wasn't that handsome." His voice was muffled as he moved his nice mouth further down my body.

More to myself than to him, I said, "I wonder what *my* credits are."

He emerged from under the bedclothes and, pretending to count, held up his index finger, considered it carefully and then, shaking his head slowly, put it back down. He repeated the same mock deliberation and rejection for each finger and when he was finished, said, "Damned if I know."

"Me either."

"Fishing for compliments then? Well, first of all, anybody can see you were once good looking. And may be again."

"And that's it?"

"You appear to be reasonably intelligent. You once had a career. Let's see. There must be something else. Oh yes. The most appealing thing about you, that first time I saw you, was that half broken-hearted, half toughing-it-out expression on your face. Pitiful but determined."

"An irresistible combination for someone like you. Especially the pitiful part. Guy, why didn't you ever marry?"

"Look at me. The ones I wanted wouldn't have me and vice versa. I had to wait for sale time – originally superior but damaged goods." He smiled.

"Spoken like a retailer." I rolled away. From my part of the bed I could see the top of a maple tree, a thick cluster of green leaves, and a patch of deep blue sky. As if to shy away from an inner screening I couldn't bear to view, my eyes had developed a tendency to blink rapidly; a tick I developed right after the shooting.

"Augie Gunther told me he had once been married. But the police could find no record of it."

"He wanted to appear as normal as possible." He was pulling me close again when, from outdoors, a voice called out, "Anybody home?"

A gale of activity blasted through the front door. Like children caught with matches, or actually exactly like grownups caught with their pants down, we sprang out of bed and pulled on underwear, tee shirts, jeans and socks. I was faster. Not bothering with shoes, I ran downstairs.

Dilly and Lorraine Thorn, hand in hand, were standing in the front foyer. Avoiding looking at the smaller of the two, I waved them in.

"We were on our way back from picking up the *Times* – we brought you a copy too – "

"Guy has his delivered."

"Oh well, Moore and I need two puzzles anyway – when Dilly suggested we stop by and say hello."

"We make you company," Dilly said. "I'm almost four. You can come to my birthday you want."

Entering the room, neat and imperturbable, and unlike me, fully shod, Guy said in astonishment, "You are almost four? I could have sworn you were five."

"I'm having growth spurts."

As usual, Dilly headed straight for the antique toy fire engine in the corner.

Guy said, "The answer is still no."

"Why?"

"I'm saving it."

'You saving it? For who?"

"My grandchildren."

"You have grandchildren?"

"Not at the moment. But who knows?"

"You fooling me." He brightened. "I know. You pretend you *my* grandfather."

"Go get your own grandfather. As a matter of fact, you're well supplied."

"We share the fire engine? Okay? I take it home. You come any time and play in my room." He considered a moment. "Your grandchild can come too."

Guy began to laugh without restraint. I watched him, wishing I could laugh like that. Not only couldn't I do it, I couldn't remember what it felt like. Would I ever?

Guy waved Lorraine to the sofa. "Coffee?"

"No thank you."

"Anything new?"

"Not really. This lawyer I got for Faith – "

"Mommy, you a lawyer. Why you not Faith's lawyer?"

"I'm not the kind she needs."

"What kind she need?"

"Criminal. As I was saying – "

"Faith a criminal?"

I answered that one. "Yes." I wasn't sure what the crime was. Killing August Gunther was not the one I had in mind.

"Because you kill the Man?"

"Well – "

"Why it bad kill the Man? He hurted me."

"Dilly, will you please shut up for a minute so I can get a word in?" Lorraine said.

"That's rude!" Dilly shouted in an outraged tone.

"Okay, I apologize. Now, if you don't mind, I'd like permission to continue."

As usual when a discussion of my trial, my chance of acquittal and my future arose, I spun my cocoon. Blurring the buzz of voices, I did what I always did when withdrawing from reality: I sketched. However, words intermittently pierced the protective envelope.

". . . killing a police officer . . . murder one . . . twenty to life . . . doesn't necessarily preclude a manslaughter indictment in case she's found innocent of murder one . . . four years minimum . . . which seems quite possible given what they'll probably find with the DNA evidence linking Gunther to the other murders . . . some hope for full acquittal . . . emotional disturbance . . . no priors . . . suffering from amnesia . . . certainly adequate provocation . . . the DNA evidence linking Gunther to the other murders will help . . . no premeditation . . . Karen might go for temporary insanity . . . ."

"Insanity mean Faith crazy?"

"Dilly dear, go play with the damned fire engine."

"You make me cry."

"Cry quietly."

The buzz continued. ". . . drag on for a year . . . advantage for the prosecution . . . at the moment people are emotional about the crime . . . we'll try to locate as many mothers as we can of the victims . . . ."

Mothers of the victims. Did they still wake up at night to the screams and pleas of their babies? Did the victims – what was left of them – stir in their tiny coffins and still cry for help?

". . . the cousin, the one who inherited after Faith disappeared, will return the money . . . will help with the costs . . . buried Bobby in a little cemetery near his home . . . when all over Faith and I will visit it . . . too bad Faith didn't wake up sooner in time to save the others . . . might visit my adopted children in Ecuador once our affairs are in order . . . ."

Once our affairs are in order.

How did one get a murdered child back in order?

"How you like to babysit me?" Dilly asked.

Reluctantly, I unglued my eyes from my sketching pad and looked into his blue ones.

"Cindy going back to school," he continued. "Mommy says she get a MA. What MA is? Mommy says it make her smarter. We can chat. I let you play with my pirate ship." He glanced meaningfully at Guy. "I share a lot."

Ignoring the hint, Guy said, "Dilly, I'm afraid Faith is going to be pretty busy. She's a volunteer at the Portland shelter – "

"What she do there?"

"She takes care of children who don't have – "

"She can take care me instead."

"The kids at the shelter need her more. And the rest of the time she's getting ready for an art show in the Fall."

"An art show?" Lorraine looked back and forth between me and the sketch pad.

"Faith used to do portraits on commission and sell her paintings through galleries and art shows."

"Want to do Dilly's portrait?"

I looked past her at the unripe apples on the tree in front of the house, at the malva and roses bordering the low stone wall, at the finch pecking at the suet in the bird house. Then I shook my head. "No."

She hesitated a moment, as if to pursue the subject, but changed her mind. Instead she said, "Another reason I came over is to invite you to Dilly's birthday party and also – "

"I got a idea." Excitedly, Dilly began jumping up and down in place, his arms flapping as if he were about to take flight. "You give me that fire engine for my birthday present."

"– to let you know you'll be getting an invitation to my wedding in September." She smiled uneasily. "So stick around."

"I'll certainly try to," I said. "The prosecutor, the judge and particularly Guy – who put a lien on his house for me for bail – might appreciate it."

"Okay?" said Dilly. "You give me the fire engine?"

"No."

"Come on, Dill Pill, maybe we can arrange for a play date with Tracy this afternoon."

Gloomily, Dilly said, "That's not my mood. To Guy: "I take it home for a little bit?"

"No."

Dilly looked down at my foot and then tucked his hand into his mother's. "You have a broken sock," he told me, and forgivingly to Guy, "Have a nice day."

"You too."

Guy was still smiling for a long time after they left. I examined him soberly. In the brightness generated by Dilly's lingering aura, he seemed to shimmer faintly, as if enveloped by a glow. I had stopped noticing his odd appearance. My vision had been affected by other considerations.

What other considerations? The enchantment of his house? The beauty of his rolling acres? His money?

I didn't think so.

He put his arms around me protectively, his grip tightening spasmod-ically as if he'd just remembered the "twenty to life" or even the "four years minimum."

When had I ever felt protected before?

Robert – Bobby' s father – was a dim memory. After only two years of marriage, he'd departed, never to return, with a pretty, blond investment banker he'd met at a convention. He hadn't been aware I was pregnant. He hadn't been aware of the gift he had left me. The horror.

We began to do our stretching exercises while we talked.

"Notice how Lorraine is always trying to give me money? Asking me to paint Dilly's portrait? Getting Dilly to suggest babysitting?"

"How about you and me making it a double wedding with Lorraine and

Moore?"

"Still trying to keep the homeless off the streets?"

"Not all. Just one."

"One small step for homeless-kind. One giant leap for Faith."

"Who would we invite to the wedding? Your cousin out west? My mother in Arizona? My father in Maine? Who knows where my brother is."

I panted as I did sit ups. "Another dysfunctional family."

"We human beings do find it hard to get along with one another."

"What makes you think you and I will be different?"

"Well, we're older for one thing. We both have what they call . . . challenges, these days. Temporary, it's true, in your case, but I have a lot of material comforts to offer you. We're both into – "

"What will you tell the neighbors when they ask about your wife if I go to jail?"

"They'll already know. Besides, the neighbors aren't my primary consideration."

"You know who that yellow dog was, the one that attacked Dilly and me?"

"Yeah?"

"It was Conrad Van Kuhn's. For a while there, I thought he might have deliberately set it loose."

"You mean you suspected him of being the killer?"

"I suspected everyone."

"Including me?"

"Sure."

His sit ups were better than mine and he wasn't panting.

"Guy, do you happen to have an empty box about the size of a purse? And some wrapping paper and tape?"

He began his push ups. "The good news is that the maximum security prison is right here in the county. Think they'll let me visit every week?"

I didn't answer.

"Why do you suppose," he continued, "that he – Augie – asked you out that night?"

I leaned against the wall and stretched my calf muscles. "I don't think it was for my 'once good looks.' Maybe he wanted to lull my suspicions. Although he was actually one of the few people I didn't suspect. Maybe he wanted to slip something into my after-the-movie drink. Keep me dormant and out of his way until he was through with Dilly."

Suddenly I was nauseated. I went to the kitchen and sipped a glass of water. Would it always be this way? Intermittent moments of peace and forgetfulness and then the return of the asphyxiating tidal wave? Would I continue to wake up in the middle of the night and hear the childish voice asking, "Do you hear a noise?" Would the torment ever abate?

Guy was standing behind me. Gently, he asked, "What was that you said about wrapping paper and an empty box?"

I put down the glass. Rubbing the skin between my eyebrows, I said, "Wait here." I went upstairs to the long corridor and, opening a lower drawer, took out the stolen purse. Back downstairs, I held it up for his inspection. "Does this look like the purse of a homeless person?"

He glanced at it without interest. "Did that come from my store?"

"I stole it."

During a lifetime that couldn't have been smooth – he must have been tormented by schoolmates while growing up, or not growing up sufficiently – Guy had learned to flatten his emotions, adjust to the bumps and move on.

"You stole it?" he asked, as if it were only to be expected.

"When I was in Boston, I was desperate to get to South Springport and I didn't have the fare so I picked up the purse of a woman who had put it down on a fruit stand. Can you lend me – I think it was five or six twenties and some singles?"

He went to his desk, took out his wallet and handed me five hundred dollars.

"It's too much."

"Interest. Compensation for mental anguish. Whatever."

As we selected a suitable box and I copied her name and address from her driver's license on a mailing label, I said, "I never saw anybody as efficient as you. Ordinarily I'm prejudiced against people who are too neat and organized – "

"Nobody's perfect."

"– but in your case it seems okay."

"My mother was a slob. I over compensated. You ready?"

"Almost." I finished wrapping, pasted on the label and left the parcel on the living room bench for mailing the next day. I ran upstairs to replace the torn sock Dilly had called "broken" and put on my new jogging shoes. Just as we were ready to start out, I looked around at the flowered sofas, the books, the bronze sculpture, the worn Oriental rug. Would I spend the rest of my life among these objects or in the maximum security prison where Guy planned on visiting me weekly?

We started out slowly down Water Wheel Road. "Guy," I said, "you never told me – I mean do you think it was wrong? What I did?"

"What I can't understand is why one of the relatives of the other kids didn't do it sooner."

"They didn't know who he was. Want me to tell you the real reason I did it?"

"Hey, cut that out. There was no reason. It was sheer insanity." He looked around as if afraid we were surrounded by eavesdroppers.

"I didn't do it for Bobby's sake."

He faltered for a moment and then doggedly continued jogging.

"The real reason I did it was to make sure Dilly would be safe."

"Yeah? Well, never repeat that to anyone else. It sounds too much like premeditation to me. That lawyer Lorraine hired for you better have some long talks with you if she plans on putting you on the stand."

"I was afraid August Gunther would get himself a slick lawyer, drown the jury with stories about his miserable childhood – "

"Which apparently he *did* have. They found his journal."

"– and get himself acquitted. He was very winning. He would have had them teary eyed. They might have forgotten that everyone, no matter how ill treated, is ultimately responsible for – "

"Hey, you're preaching to the choir." He picked up the pace as if to get away from this discussion and I tried not to lag behind.

"– his own actions. Otherwise, we could all justify everything we do by blaming our fathers or our second grade teachers or the man next door who – "

"I agree."

"Then you don't blame me for shooting him?"

He was silent.

"You do blame me?"

"Well – I could never blame you, Faith. On the other hand, I'm not sure, that as a general principle, I believe in sidestepping all that trial by jury business and just lynching people – "

"But in so many cases, people like August Gunther are declared insane – " I waved at a passing car. The driver waved back, "– sent to a mental institution for a year or two and then released. I was afraid he would come back for Dilly."

"Speaking of whom – " Guy was beginning to pant. "I need – your advice. Do you – think – I ought to give – that damn fire truck to Dilly after all?"

THE END

Acknowledgements

Mildred Davis is the author of this book and my mother. I helped in the editing of the book and made certain changes to place the book in a location and time different from the original.

We are blessed with many family and friends who made other substantial contributions to this book. The cover of this book (as well as that of *Murder in Maine: The Avenging of Nevah Wright* also by Mildred Davis and Katherine Roome) is graced with a painting by George Van Hook of Cambridge, New York. Susie Weil of Bedford, New York, contributed all of Faith's sketches except for two. The two sketches which precede Chapters 3 and 7 were created by Tom St. Laurent of Greenwich New York. We have Jimmy Lannon of Freeport, Maine to thank for everything that is accurate about certain aspects of MidCoast Maine. Our most grateful thanks goes to Dr. Don Goff of Boston Massachusetts for geographical details in Boston as well as certain details concerning Faith's circumstances as a homeless person. Thanks to Darcy May of Greenwich, New York for the map of South Springport. We have Chris Lapham and Frank Barbolla, both of Greenwich New York, to thank for everything that is accurate about the police work in this book. We have Pamela Davis, Mildred's daughter and my sister (and a former prosecutor), to thank for details regarding Faith's crime and the prosecution thereof. Amy Davis, another of my sisters, provided timely proofreading assistance. Our thanks to Hugh Roome, my husband, for the cover design and invaluable marketing tips. Thanks to Ellie DeVries of Greenwich, New York for her contribution to our description of South Freeport Express.

Our most grateful thanks to Denise Film for her help in proofreading and production assistance. And our thanks to Jim Russo at Channel One Design, Inc. for his able assistance in designing the book.

Finally, our loving thanks to two contributors who unknowingly made major contributions to this manuscript almost 15 years ago. The first is Tyler DeAngelo of New York, NY, Mildred's grandson and my nephew. Tyler created Skip's drawings when he was fourteen years old (although I hasten to add that, notwithstanding the seemingly psychotic nature of these drawings, Tyler is a gentle, sane soul who has nothing in common with the character whose drawings he created). And finally, our thanks to Ren

Roome, my son and another of Mildred's grandsons who, as a four year old, unwittingly contributed Dilly's drawings and much of Dilly's syntax and expressions. It was a four year old Ren who asked, after Mildred had described to him the manner in which chickens are raised, butchered, fricasseed and eaten, "Does the chicken like it?"

Did we forget anyone? We most fervently hope not although, as should be evident from this list, there would be no book without the help of many friends.

Katherine Roome
Greenwich, NY
2007

Mildred Davis is the author of fourteen mystery novels, including *They Buried a Man* (Simon & Schuster), *The Voice on the Telephone* (Random House), *Three Minutes To Midnight* (Random House), and *The Room Upstairs* (Simon & Schuster) which won the Mystery Writers of America Edgar Allan Poe Award. Her daughter, Katherine Roome, is the author of *Letter of the Law* (Random House), and co-author with her mother of *Murder In Maine: The Avenging of Nevah Wright* (HARK LLC) and *Lucifer Land* (Random House), an historical novel set in Westchester County during the Revolutionary War. Mildred Davis lives in Westchester County, New York and Katherine Roome lives in Washington County, New York.

To order additional copies of this book
or other books by the authors, contact:

HARK LLC
www.harkpublishing.com

FROM THE SAME AUTHORS

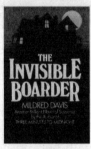

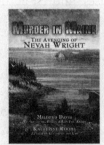